"This is all your fault," Tisha accused

"Why did you let dad bully you into agreeing to marry me?"

"Guilt, I suppose," Roarke answered calmly.

"Guilt?" she flared. "There was nothing to be guilty about! Nothing happened!"

"You're right. Physically nothing happened." An eyebrow quirked as his gaze roamed over her. "But in my mind, let's say that it didn't end with kisses, little girl."

"We're getting...off the track," Tisha stammered, turning away from him.

His hands settled around her waist in a provocative caress. "I thought we were on the track." He nuzzled her neck. "We're engaged. We should enjoy some of the pleasures that go along with it."

Tisha gulped. "You forget we're trying to find a way out of this engagement."

"Are we?" he asked. Then his mouth came down on hers....

JANET DAILEY AMERICANA

VALLEY
OF THE VAPOURS

Harlequin Books

TORONTO • NEW YORK • LONDON
AMSTERDAM • PARIS • SYDNEY • HAMBURG
STOCKHOLM • ATHENS • TOKYO • MILAN

The state flower depicted on the cover of this book is apple blossom.

Janet Dailey Americana edition published July 1986
Second printing March 1988
Third printing April 1989

ISBN 373-21904-0

Harlequin Presents edition published March 1977

Original hardcover edition published in 1976
by Mills & Boon Limited

Printed in U.S.A.

CHAPTER ONE

'WHAT do you mean you gave Kevin Jamieson permission to marry me?' Tisha Caldwell demanded angrily. Long hair flew about her shoulders at the sudden pivot that brought her glaring eyes to bear on her father.

'I gave him permission to ask you to marry him.' His reply was drawn through tightly clenched teeth.

'With your full support and blessing!' she finished, not attempting to disguise the caustic sarcasm rising so bitterly in her throat.

They stared at one another, two forceful personalities, each trying to make the other give in first. Richard Caldwell was a tall, handsome man with a muscular physique that hadn't varied one inch since his college days. The years had only added character to his already handsome face and some dignified feathers of grey to his dark hair.

Tisha Caldwell did not have the striking looks of her father. In repose, her oval face was only ordinarily attractive. But when animated by laughter or anger, as now, she was compellingly beautiful. Her inheritance of her father's volatile personality and stubborn independence made the flashes of beauty occur frequently. And most of the time, it was her father who ignited the sparks.

'Yes, Kevin received my support and my blessing,' Richard Caldwell retorted sharply, his temper rising in conjunction with what he labelled his daughter's insolence. 'He's a respectable and respectful young man, which is more than I can say for those other "things" you go out with!'

'He certainly isn't like any of the other boys I date!' Tisha agreed fervently. 'I get the feeling when he kisses me goodnight, he runs home to take a shower in case he's got dirty.'

'I assure you he is a normal healthy male who merely has his emotions under control.' His index finger was pointed in an angry gesture towards her. 'At least you don't come in from a date looking as if you've been pawed by some over-sexed beast when you are out with Kevin.'

Her hands doubled up into fists. 'You make me so angry I could scream,' was her muttered answer. 'Only a couple of the boys I've gone out with have ever stepped out of line. None of my dates have ever made a practice of pawing me, as you put it.'

'You're darn right they don't!' he snapped, his brown eyes snapping with anger as he stared into the stormy sea green ones of his daughter. 'Because before they ever leave this house with you, they know they're going to have to face me if they so much as lay a finger on you!'

'I'll be twenty years old next month, Father,' Tisha sighed in exasperation. 'Will you stop treating me like a child? I'm old enough to decide if I'm going to marry and whom I'm going to marry without any advice from you. I'm capable of deciding whom I will date and defending myself if necessary!'

'No woman can defend herself against the superior strength of a man,' he scoffed with an authoritative ring of personal knowledge in his voice. 'It's up to her father and subsequently her husband to protect her.'

'Oh, heavens, that sounds like something from the Dark Ages! That chauvinistic attitude went out with the Ark,' she grumbled.

'It's time it made a nostalgic comeback,' Richard Caldwell muttered. He was about to expound further when the doorbell rang.

Tisha darted a baleful glance at him. 'I suppose you told Kevin to come round this afternoon,' she accused. 'All I can say is I certainly hope he didn't waste his money buying me a ring, although it would give me great satisfaction to throw it in his face.'

'You keep a civil tongue in your head, girl!' A finger again waved angrily in the direction of her back as Tisha stomped around the room divider to the mock foyer of the front door.

With an impatient hand she swept her dark auburn, nearly waist-length hair behind her back as she flung the door open, ready to lash out with her tongue at the man she expected to see on the stoop. The woman standing there arched an inquisitive glance when Tisha's mouth snapped shut in a grim line. A bemused smile tilted the corners of the woman's mouth.

'I have the feeling I should come back another time.'

7

Brown eyes glittered with laughter.

Tisha stepped away from the door, the movement allowing the woman to enter, which she did. Crinkling laugh lines were around her eyes and combined with the faint wrinkles on her forehead and throat indicated the woman's age to be more than the first glance would suggest. The feathery cap of short dark hair possessed a startling streak of white that looked artificial unless the hair roots were examined.

Tisha didn't wait for the woman to follow as she left the slender woman standing inside the door while she stalked back around the divider.

'It's only Blanche,' answering the unasked question in her father's arched brows, not sure whether she was sorry or glad that it wasn't Kevin as she sank into the cushions of the flowered sofa.

The muscles in his jaw jumped convulsively, signalling that his anger, like Tisha's, seethed just below the surface. 'You will address your aunt as your aunt and not some acquaintance,' her father growled. 'You will show respect for your elders.'

'If she calls me Aunt Blanche, I'll clobber both of you!' But laughter still lurked behind the sternly voiced reprimand as Blanche Caldwell walked around the divider.

In her bright red slacks and equally bright red and white flowered blouse, she looked the complete opposite of what a spinster aunt was supposed to be like. Unmindful of her brother's quelling look, Blanche Caldwell covered the short distance that separated them and planted a quick kiss on his cheek.

'And I'm delighted to see you, too, Richard,' she said dryly.

'I'm glad you are here,' he said emphatically, shifting his position slightly so his gaze could take in his sister and his daughter. 'I'm trying to talk some sense into this girl's head and she won't listen to me.'

'Sense!' A bitter sound that bore little resemblance to laughter came from Tisha. A hand waved airily in her father's direction. 'He's trying to convince me that I should marry some man who gives me the creeps simply because he's decent!'

'I am not trying to force you to marry Kevin Jamieson!' her father shouted.

'What do you call it, then?' she demanded.

'Do you see what I mean?' Richard Caldwell turned to his sister, his hands raised in a frustrated, beseeching gesture for understanding. 'She deliberately twists everything around, puts words in my mouth that aren't even there. I only said he was a nice boy and that she could do worse.'

'No matter who *I* picked to marry, Dad, you wouldn't be able to stand them. You'd find something wrong with them even if it was only the colour of their eyes.' Now it was Tisha who turned to Blanche. 'He doesn't believe a woman is capable of knowing what or who is good for her. It's his responsibility to interfere in my life!'

'Considering the type of boys you go out with, it's no wonder that I feel the need to step in once in a while,' he replied quickly. 'Most of your dates only have one thing in mind, and if I didn't play the heavy-handed father waiting with the shotgun, they probably would have got it.'

'If you had your way, I wouldn't date anybody until you found the man you wanted me to marry,' Tisha retorted. 'You try to tell me what clothes to wear, how much make-up to put on, who my friends should be. Why won't you accept the fact that I'm an adult?'

'That's because you don't act like one!'

'Only because you don't let me,' leaning forward to enforce her words. 'When we sit down to a meal, you still ask if I washed my hands. I'm not a child!'

Blanche Caldwell had been watching the interchange silently, her gaze shifting from one to the other like a spectator at a tennis match.

'Oh, Richard, you don't do that, do you?' she laughed softly.

He looked momentarily disgruntled. 'Well, sometimes she forgets to wash the oil paint from her hands and it makes the food smell bad,' he mumbled gruffly.

'How many times have I done that?' Tisha demanded. 'Once? Twice? Not more than that, I know.'

'We're getting away from the topic of this conversation,' her father stated, shifting his weight from one foot to the other.

'No, we are not!' Tisha affirmed angrily. 'We're talking about the way you're trying to run my life! The way you keep dictating what I wear, who I see and where I go!'

'I'm your father. I have a right to do it.'

'And I'm a person with a right to some privacy and to make my own mistakes!' Strange olive green flames burned in her eyes, opened wide so the thick, dark lashes didn't veil her wrath.

'As long as you live in my house and eat my food, I have some say in the matter.'

'Well, maybe that's the solution,' Tisha stated coldly. 'Maybe I should just move out.'

'You can think again, young lady,' but there was a substantial subsiding of his anger. 'You aren't earning enough money to live on your own and I still control the small trust fund your mother set up for you until you're twenty-one. Without that income, you'd be lucky if there was any food in your hand when it got to your mouth, not on what little you make.'

'I'm beginning to understand what oppression is. I'd almost rather starve to death than to live under this roof where you can order me around!' she cried out bitterly.

'If you're going to persist in talking to me with that kind of disrespect, you can go to your room.' His face was being drawn into grimmer and sterner lines as he made a superhuman effort to control his temper.

'I'm not a child. I won't be ordered to my room as though I were!' For all the outward show of defiance, there was an inward cringing at the fury in her father's face.

'Patricia Jo Caldwell, you're not too old to be taken

over my knee,' he threatened.

A laughing sigh from Blanche spliced the crackling air between father and daughter. 'You're ten years too late with that remedy, Richard.' Her gaze twinkled sympathetically towards her brother, then moved to her niece with a warm, understanding light in their depths.

A disgusted frown marred the handsome face. 'What else are you supposed to do with a headstrong, rebellious child like mine?' he asked absently. 'If her mother was alive, maybe she could reason with her. I'm only trying to do what I feel is best.'

'But what about what I feel, Dad?' Tisha demanded, the mention of her mother dulling the sharpness in her voice.

'If you'd listen once in a while instead of arguing all the time,' Richard Caldwell began. only to close his mouth on the rest of the statement. 'You never were one to take advice. You always had to find out for yourself whether the fire was hot.'

'It could be a case of like father, like daughter,' Blanche suggested quietly.

'Heaven forbid!' Tisha declared, rising to her feet.

'Where are you going?' demanded Richard Caldwell.

'To my room, because *I*,' adding emphasis to the word, 'want to go there. And if Kevin calls, tell him the answer is no, I'll never marry him. Nor do I ever want to see him again!'

'I never said you had to!' Frustration mixed with his

anger to wring the declaration from his throat.

Tisha paused in the doorway, half-turning to look over her shoulder at the handsome man who was her father. Her back was still arched, but some of the turbulence had gone from her sea green eyes.

'No, Dad, you never order me to do anything,' she agreed grimly. 'You use charm and emotional blackmail until I find myself in a situation like this where you've led a man that you know I don't care for to believe that I would consider marrying him. It's always what *you* think is best for me.'

'Is that so wrong?' he demanded, but with the suggestion of wheedling charm in his voice as he managed a conciliatory smile. 'You haven't really given Kevin a chance. In time, you may find that you'll grow to love him.'

A sadly wistful smile curved her mouth. 'You won't give up, will you? I mean it, Dad. I can't and I won't marry him. If I ever marry, and I'm beginning to seriously doubt that I'll ever want to, it will be to someone I choose and you'll have nothing to say about it.'

'Don't be absurd!' A frown creased his forehead. 'Of course you're going to get married. What other future does a woman have? A husband and children are the ultimate fulfilment for a woman.'

'Is that right?' There was a mocking lift of Tisha's brow. 'I think Blanche would disagree with you. I don't think I've ever seen any wife and mother as content as your sister is with her life and career. I envy Blanche her freedom. Not even you try to dictate to her.'

This time Tisha didn't give her father an opportunity to reply as she stepped into the hallway that led to her room, knowing this was the moment to end the argument when the last point was hers. Blanche's untrammelled laughter followed her, as did her father's sputtering anger.

A few seconds after Tisha had entered her room, there was a light rap on the door. 'Come in, Blanche,' she called.

The older woman's face wore a smile of half-humorous understanding when she walked into the room. Tisha's lightning-quick temper that had lent voice to her anger had vanished, but the deep-seated look of rebellion was still there.

'I'd apologize for that unpleasant scene you just witnessed,' Tisha spoke, 'but you've known your brother a lot longer than I have.'

The brown cap of curling hair moved downward in a nod of agreement. 'There are times when Richard can be overbearingly male,' Blanche acknowledged. 'A case of too many females pandering to his ego in the past.'

'Including me,' Tisha sighed, picking up a jacket tossed over a chair and walking across the bold orange and gold tweed carpet to hang it in her wardrobe. The decor of the room was a reflection of her own gregarious personality, sunny and bright with bold splashes of colour. 'When I was growing up, he was Mr. Everything – strong, and powerful, loving and kind, handsome with a touch of the rugged individualist about him. I used to dream of meeting a man just like him.' A wry grimace chased across her face. 'Thank goodness I never did! Now I understand why Mom and Dad used to fight so much.'

'As I recall,' her aunt said idly, wandering into the small alcove of the bedroom remodelled to serve as a private studio for Tisha, 'those arguments between Lenore and your father always ended in laughter and kisses. A weaker woman couldn't have brought him the happiness he knew with your mother. Richard couldn't dominate her. That's why he loved her.'

'Well, I wish he'd stop trying to dominate me!'

Blanche smiled. 'I don't believe he'll ever succeed at it. You're too much like your father and your mother.'

'Why can't he see that? Why can't he accept that I know my own mind?' she demanded.

'There are two reasons for that, Tish. The first and underlying cause is that reformed rogues always make the strictest parents. And my brother sowed a lot of wild oats before he met Lenore.' She paused to watch the acceptance of her words revealed on her niece's face and continued when she received the recognition. 'Secondly, the loss of your mother when you were only fourteen increased Richard's sense of responsibility towards you. He knows he can't take your mother's place, but he feels he must actively involve himself in your life, more so than if your mother was alive or if you had an aunt that only showed up when it suited her.'

'Oh, Blanche!' A radiant smile immediately took possession of her features. 'I wouldn't have any other aunt but you. You always seem to be here when I need someone to talk to, to put all my little problems in their proper perspective.'

'I'm glad I can be helpful once in a while.'

'You are,' Tisha affirmed. 'Now tell me, what brings you out of your Ozark Mountain hideaway in Hot Springs all the way to Little Rock? I'm sure you didn't come to act as a referee for me and my father.'

'I'm using the excuse that I came to pick up art supplies.' There was a smile teasing the corners of her mouth. 'But I was really motivated by a sense of guilt that it had been too long since I'd seen my family – you and Richard. I tend to lose track of time.'

'It wasn't much of a welcome we gave you.' Chagrin clouded the green eyes looking into the gentle brown light of her aunt's gaze.

'I hope I haven't been gone so long that I require trumpet fanfares and red carpets,' Blanche laughed easily. As if to change the conversation away from herself, the slender woman turned to the array of paintings haphazardly scattered about the alcove. 'Your father intimated that you weren't having much financial success in your work.'

'That is unfortunately true,' Tisha sighed, walking over to stand beside her aunt, 'at least in the paintings that I do for my own satisfaction. I'm slowly coming to the conclusion that I'm commercially adequate but not artistically unique. My brush doesn't have the stroke of genius behind it directing it the way yours does.'

Blanche studied a nostalgic still life depicting an old

butter churn sitting in the corner of a wooden porch where sunflowers bobbed their golden heads above the railing.

'There's nothing wrong with being a commercial artist, Tisha. What have you been selling?'

'Some greeting cards and calendars, but mostly it's been advertisements.' Grimness pulled at her mouth. 'Dad was right, you know, I'm not earning enough money to make it on my own. However much I'd like to have a place of my own I would be dependent on my father's benevolence.'

With a frustrated movement, she pushed her long hair behind her ear. The silken tresses caught the sunlight streaming in the window, transforming the colour that appeared to be a simple auburn under artificial lights into a fiery golden-red shade.

'Sometimes I wish I'd been born a man,' Tisha declared. Her voice vibrated with a disguised anger. 'A woman is controlled by her parents until she marries. Then she's a slave to her husband's whims for the rest of her life. I think I hate all men. The way they've tried to convince us that they're so much better than women is sickening. We are the weaker sex because we were given less muscle and more brains. A woman can outwit a man any day.'

Dark eyes glinted in Tisha's direction. 'Who's disillusioned you about the male sex? This Kevin boy or your father?'

'I think it's a combination of every male I've known,' Tisha replied, bitterly serious and cynical.

"Someone once told me that to get a man to like you all you had to do was listen and only open your mouth to ask questions about him. Men want a girl to be attractive but silent. They don't care what her accomplishments or talents are. They always act as if they're doing you a favour by asking you for a date.'

'You've been reading too many of those feminist pamphlets,' Blanche scolded her mildly. 'Men and women are first of all human beings, each possessing their own faults. You aren't trying to tell me that there haven't been a few boys you've liked, are you?'

A sheepish grin spread over Tisha's face as she realized how pompously superior she had sounded. 'Actually there've been more than a few,' she admitted frankly, 'but I've never fooled myself into believing that I was in love with any of them. That's probably why I never raised too much fuss when Dad would put his foot down on going out with one of them. But I won't allow him to tell me who I'm going to marry.'

'For all his arrogant interference, Richard is concerned about your happiness, although I do agree that he has a poor way of showing it,' her aunt agreed. 'Now that he knows how totally you oppose this Kevin, he won't force you to see him.'

'Not Kevin. He'll find someone else,' Tisha grumbled. Her hands flew about the air in a hopeless, beseeching gesture. 'I love my father dearly, Blanche, but I just can't live with him. As long as I do, he's going to persist in trying to manage my life. I suppose the only thing I can do is give up painting and get a job.'

18

'I have another idea that might work,' Blanche told her, turning back to look at more of her niece's paintings. 'You could move to Hot Springs and live with me.'

'Seriously?' Tisha breathed, unable to believe that she had heard correctly. Blanche Caldwell was notoriously protective of her privacy and solitude.

'Yes, seriously,' her aunt nodded, meeting the questioning eyes with calm assurance. 'If you want a career in art, there isn't any need to sacrifice your work because of money and a stubborn father.'

'But what will Dad say?'

'How can he openly oppose his own sister acting as chaperon?' Blanche laughed, a deep throaty laugh to match her low-pitched voice.

'What about ... I mean ... will I interfere with your work?' asked Tisha, blurting out the thought that was uppermost in her mind.

'I'm a person who enjoys being alone by myself. I live that way for preference.' There was a faint smile in the otherwise serious face. 'That's not to say I'm temperamental. I could paint in the middle of the busiest intersection and never notice the traffic. I think I might enjoy having a fellow artist staying with me, especially since she's my niece.'

'What can I say?' Tisha cried, elated by the sudden turn of events that couldn't help but meet with her father's approval. In spite of all their arguments, she didn't want to alienate her father's affections by openly rebelling and leaving home without his sanction.

'If you'd like to stay with me then say "yes". It's as simple as that. I'll handle your father,' Blanche assured her. 'Of course, your social life will probably suffer until you can get acquainted.'

'If you mean by social life dating, then I don't think I will mind a break. Maybe abstinence will improve my image of the male sex. Lately everyone I've dated always seem to turn out to be so immature and self-centred.'

The laughter sounded again as Blanche closed her hand over Tisha's. 'What you need, dear, is a little affair with an older man. Remind me to introduce you to my neighbour.'

'Don't let Dad hear you say something like that,' she grinned, 'or he'll never let me stay with you.'

'It's rather unjust the way fathers especially those who've lost their mates, have no qualms about having an affair with a woman, but they insist that their daughters be good little girls,' her aunt declared with a decided twinkle in her eye. 'Not that I'm advocating that you have an affair. Aunts have their prejudices, too, although we're not nearly as straitlaced as parents.'

'What does that mean?' Tisha teased. 'That the porch light goes on twenty minutes after my date drives up to bring me home instead of Dad's usual five minutes?'

'Something like that,' Blanche laughed, squeezing her niece's hand lightly before releasing it. 'Now I must go persuade your father that it's his idea that you come stay with me. You aren't the only one who panders to his ego!'

CHAPTER TWO

Two days after Blanche's departure, Tisha was en route to her aunt's house outside of Hot Springs, Arkansas. Her compact Mustang car was jammed with clothes, paints, canvases, and every other personal possession she couldn't bear to leave behind. The lightness of her heart had nothing to do with being released from under her father's dominating thumb. It was a result of the loving farewell from her father. It had almost made Tisha wish she weren't leaving. Almost.

Autumn was beginning to make its vivid mark on the forested Ozark hills, splashing gold and scarlet colours on the leaves of the trees. Only the pines remained for ever green as a direct contrast to the autumn hues. The sun shone brightly in a milky blue sky, but there was a nip in the wind that blew from the north.

Tisha had only been to her aunt's house twice since Blanche had moved into it less than a year ago, but her memory of the route through the back roads was faultless. At a crossroads of the tree-lined country road, she slowed her blue compact to a stop, remembering the intersection clearly because of the winding road that curled up the mountain, its almost immediate curve preventing Tisha from seeing any oncoming traffic. It was the road she had to take to her aunt's house. Luckily there was rarely any traffic on these back roads, so she felt very secure in pulling into the intersection and making the turn on to the winding road.

Just as she completed the turn, an expensive foreign sports car came roaring around the curve, taking more than its share of her side of the road. There was no place for her to go to avoid the oncoming car as the hillside fell steeply away on her side. Only skilful driving on the part of the other driver saved them from a head-on collision, clipping her front bumper as he swerved by.

For a split second after she had braked her car to a halt, Tisha sat frozen behind the wheel, paralysed by the narrow miss that had left her unharmed but shaken. Slowly she unclenched her white fingers from their death grip on the wheel, a trembling rage taking possession of her at the reckless driver who could have got them both killed. The white sports car had stopped near the crossroads.

Tisha bounded out of her car, the sunlight setting her hair afire to match the anger burning in her green eyes. Long legs carried her with a striding gait down the slight incline to the car and the man just stepping out of it.

An ignited temper issued forth a stream of angry words. 'You imbecile! What were you doing coming around that corner so fast? You could have got us both killed!' Tisha shouted. 'Didn't you realize there was an intersection on the other side of the curve, or did you think because you drove a flashy car you had the right of way and the right to be on my side of the road! People like you shouldn't be allowed behind the wheel!'

Tisha was five foot six, but she had to tilt her head back to look into the face of the man who was easily two inches over six feet tall. His strong features were set in a serious expression, but his brown eyes gave the impression that he was smiling at her. Her heart began beating at a rapid tempo, an after-effect of the accident, no doubt.

'After that vigorous tirade, you can't have been harmed.' His low-pitched, slightly husky voice had a very pleasing sound, but Tisha was too incensed to notice.

'No thanks to you!' she retorted sharply, swinging her head in an angry gesture that sent her hair flying about her shoulders. 'You must have been doing seventy when you came around that bend. And people talk about the idiotic way women drive!'

'Hardly seventy,' he said complacently, 'or I never would have been able to avoid hitting you head-on.'

'If you hadn't been going so fast and on my side of the road, you wouldn't have hit me at all,' Tisha reminded him curtly.

'This is essentially a private road used only by the people who live on the mountain. I didn't expect to meet anyone.' His gaze was moving leisurely over the blue denim slack suit she was wearing.

She bridled visibly at his arrogant statement. 'That's no excuse for reckless driving!'

'You're quite right, Red,' he agreed smoothly, reaching out to capture her elbow with a darkly tanned hand. 'Let's go see what damage I've done to your car.'

He had turned her half around before Tisha realized what was happening and she quickly jerked her arm free, not missing the mocking line of one eyebrow he directed at her action. One darting glance at the sandy brown hair bleached nearly blond by the sun and the attractively carved features of his ruggedly handsome face warned her that he was a man accustomed to charming his way out of situations. He would soon find that she wasn't the type to fall victim to his considerable persuasions. She put on her coldest expression as she fell into step beside him.

'You have your car pretty well packed,' he commented as he walked past it to examine the front. 'Are you moving somewhere around here?'

'That's my business,' she replied with what she thought was cutting sarcasm, but his mouth twitched in amusement.

He was really quite insufferable, Tisha thought as she watched him while he surveyed the damage to her car. He was wearing an expensive brown suede suit of genuine leather that made much of his lean, muscular build. His blondish brown hair was thick and inclined to wave, but his waywardness seemed to suit the slightly untamed look about him. There was a suggestion of a cleft in the chin that jutted out to emphasize the unrelenting hardness only hinted at in the rest of his features. At a guess, Tisha judged him to be in his early mid-thirties with no wedding ring on his finger, if that was anything to go by.

'There doesn't seem to be any damage done except to your bumper,' he announced, closing the bonnet of her car. His brown eyes had a knowing gleam in them when he met her gaze as if he knew he had been subjected to her scrutiny. 'A good body repair man should be able to take care of it easily. If you're going to be in the area, I can give you the name of a local man who could do it for you.'

'The way you drive you have, no doubt, needed his services in the past,' she murmured with cloying sweetness.

'There have been one or two occasions when I've had him do work for me,' the man admitted without really admitting anything.

'I'll bet there have,' she snapped acidly, assuming her former aggressiveness. 'Do you get a commission for all the business you direct his way?'

His gaze narrowed slightly sending her pulse leaping with an unknown fear. 'As you put it earlier, Red, that's my business,' he replied, his mouth moving into a cryptic smile.

Tisha chose to ignore his rebuke. 'That's the second time you've called me that,' she said sharply. 'My name is not Red.'

'It isn't?' His brown eyes glittered over the auburn highlights in her hair made coppery bright by the sun. 'What's your name?' At the closed expression stealing over her face, he added quickly and mockingly, 'For the benefit of my insurance company, of course.'

Tisha hesitated, wishing she didn't have to tell this arrogant stranger anything about herself while knowing that it was true that he would need her name for his insurance company.

'Patricia Caldwell,' she admitted grudgingly.

'Patricia,' he repeated, letting the name roll slowly out of his mouth as though he were savouring the sound of it.

The complacent regard of his gaze as he let it roam over her was a bit unnerving, but Tisha refused to submit to the sudden rush of heat. She guessed that most women would be fascinated by his smile.

'My friends call me Tisha,' she announced coldly, 'but you may call me Miss Caldwell.'

'Miss, not Ms,' he commented with a mocking widening of his eyes. 'And you struck me as the type seeking equality of the sexes.'

'I have no desire to be equal to a man,' Tisha replied. Her chin lifted to a haughty angle. 'I don't wish to stoop to his level.'

He tossed his head back and laughed heartily. 'You're a termagant worthy of Petruchio!'

'Which makes me grateful that Shakespeare paired him with Katharina, because I have no wish to be "tamed" or dominated by a man.' Her olive dark eyes were emitting fiery sparks.

'What a pity,' he murmured, the laughter still dancing in his eyes. 'It might have been an interesting challenge.'

'Shall we dispense with the personal comments and get down to the problem at hand, namely the damage to my car?' Tisha requested sarcastically. 'I'll need the name and policy number of your insurance company.'

One side of his mouth twitched again with ill-concealed amusement, but he reached inside his jacket pocket and withdrew a leather-encased tablet and a pen. She watched the quick, sure strokes of the pen as it flew across the paper before he tore it off and gave it to her.

'My name and telephone number is there also should you need to contact me,' he said.

Unwillingly Tisha glanced at it, the bold slashes spelling out the name Roarke Madison followed by a telephone number and his insurance company.

'Are you relieved that my name isn't Petruchio?' he taunted softly.

'My only concern is getting my car repaired,' she flashed.

As usual her caustic words had little effect on him as he added smoothly, 'It would be a good idea to get that bumper taken care of as soon as possible. It's rubbing the tyre and it will eventually ruin it.'

'I'm quite capable of seeing that it gets fixed.'

There was an expressive lift of his shoulders. 'My offer still stands if you want the name of a reputable bodyshop. I wouldn't like to see you get taken by some sharp repairman.'

'What you mean is that you wouldn't like to see your insurance company get taken or your friend lose some business.'

There was a small silence as the man named Roarke Madison slowly walked from the damaged front bumper, ignored Tisha as he went by and stopped behind her to lean a hand on the roof of the car.

'The repairs shouldn't be very costly,' he said as she turned around to face him. His eyes were watching her with a lazy kind of insolence. 'Do I look as if I'm in need of the small pittance my supposed share of the take would be?'

Her mouth was closed in a grim line. Silently she admitted that money seemed to be the least of his worries. There was a decided look of affluence about him, but it only served to anger her.

'I really wouldn't know,' she shrugged, averting her head to show him she wasn't the least bit interested in his financial status – or in him. 'Since my dealings will be with your insurance company, not you, I couldn't care less.'

'Is that right?' The mockery in his voice made it a taunt. 'I thought you might be deliberately attempting to provoke me.'

Outrage flamed in the darting look she tossed at him. 'Of all the conceited male egos I've known, yours tops the list! Are you always so disgustingly sure that your looks and charm can overwhelm any opposition?'

Tisha was so busy directing freezing scorn at the narrowed brown eyes, she didn't notice the movement he made in her direction. 'I excused your initial bad temper,' he said quietly, 'because I knew you'd been shaken by the near collision. I've very willingly admitted that I was at fault, nor have I attempted to contest the fact. But I have no intention of letting you keep taking these cheap shots at me.'

At the conclusion of the softly spoken threat, Tisha discovered his arms were on either side of her, pinning her against the car, and his face was uncomfortably close to hers. Her mouth was suddenly very dry.

'What are you doing?' she demanded, hating the fear that had crept into her voice as she moulded her body against the metal barrier of the car.

'I'm reminding you that we're on a relatively deserted country road.' A humourless smile was on his face.

'So?' was her weakly defiant reply.

'So, in a sense, you're at my mercy.' His gaze moved to her lips, slightly parted by her apprehension.

'Don't be ridiculous,' she spat, regaining some of her earlier anger. 'I'll never be at any man's mercy, least of all yours!'

'I don't know what card games you've played, but in the ones I know a king takes a queen every time. You might do well to remember that,' he mocked.

His hand moved downward on the car and her muscles tensed as Tisha prepared to fight off his advance. A metallic click broke her concentration. She glanced instinctively in the direction of the sound, startled to see the car door swinging open. Warily she looked back at the man standing so closely in front of her.

'On your way, Little Red Riding Hood.' His eyes were laughing at her disbelieving expression. 'Or the wolf may decide to eat you after all.'

Tisha needed no second invitation as she slid behind the wheel of her car, too grateful to be escaping his unwanted attention to care that she was the one doing the retreating. She didn't waste a backward look as she put the car in gear and accelerated around the curve and out of sight.

A few minutes later Tisha was turning her car into the pillared driveway of her aunt. The house was perched on a hillside overlooking a verdant forested valley on the south. At first glance, it was an unimposing structure of unfinished cedar pine, rustic and in keeping with its setting. The sun glinting on the rooftop windows of the wing was an indication of the house's totally modern interior.

There was no sign of Blanche as Tisha parked the car and climbed out. She started to reach into the back seat for some of her things when the sound of a stone rolling in the gravel turned her back around. A black and white spotted goat was staring at her, little nubbins of horns beginning to appear on its head, and a hint of a beard beneath his chin.

'Where did you come from?' she smiled.

In answer the goat shook its head in a threatening gesture and Tisha noticed the intimidating look in his eyes. He quite obviously believed her to be trespassing and though his horns were not yet fully formed, she didn't want to be attacked by the butting head. Taking

30

care not to make any sudden movement that might antagonize him, she reached into the open window of her car and sounded the horn. She didn't take her eyes off the goat when she heard the opening of the front door.

'Is he a friend of yours, Blanche?' she asked hesitantly.

'You've met my gardener,' Blanche laughed.

At the sound of her aunt's voice, the goat turned his head from Tisha, emitting a stuttering baaah.

'Run along, Gruff,' Blanche instructed. 'Tisha has come to stay with us.'

As though he understood every word, the goat cast one brief glance in Tisha's direction before wandering off.

'That is your gardener?' Tisha queried, widening her eyes as she gave her aunt a look that plainly doubted her sanity.

'I don't have much of a yard,' shrugged Blanche, an unmistakable twinkle in her eyes, 'but I needed something to keep the weeds down, so I acquired Gruff. He thinks he's a watchdog as well.'

'He did a very excellent job of convincing me that he was.' Tisha stared after the goat, now contentedly munching some grass near the fence. 'What did you call him? Gruff? It's a very good name for him.'

'Billy was a bit too trite,' Blanche smiled. 'I remembered a fairy tale I heard as a child and named him Billy Goat Gruff. He makes a very useful pet. He's quite affectionate at times.'

31

There was a doubting look in the glance Tisha cast at Blanche. 'I hope his affection will stretch to include me.'

'He's only gruff with strangers, if you'll pardon the pun,' her aunt assured her. 'Once he gets to know you, you'll be able to come and go as you please. The very fact that he's ignoring you now indicates that he has accepted you. Sometimes he simply hangs around when I have visitors, peering into the windows and lurking around corners. He rather unnerves them.'

'He does fit the image of a pet to an eccentric artist, doesn't he?' Tisha teased.

'Do you think so?' Blanche asked in an amused voice. 'Probably he does. Well, shall we get your car unloaded and your things moved into the house. I've rearranged my studio so you can have part of it to work in.'

'You didn't need to do that,' Tisha protested.

'I have plenty of room for myself,' her aunt insisted as she picked up a pair of suitcases. 'How did Richard take your leaving?'

'He wasn't happy about it, but he seemed reconciled that it was the best solution.' A wistful expression tugged downward the corners of Tisha's mouth. 'The house will probably seem very empty and lonely to him now.'

'Don't go feeling sorry for him. You would be leaving home sooner or later and he knows it. It's just as well that he becomes used to it now. Besides, living alone isn't so bad. I ought to know.'

'I'm not considering moving back,' Tisha declared. 'It would only be a matter of days before Dad and I would be fighting over something. I just hope I won't be in your way too much.'

'You won't. If I thought you might, I would never have invited you.' Blanche smiled reassuringly as she opened the door of her house for Tisha to enter. 'How was the drive here?'

Tisha's nose wrinkled in disgruntled remembrance. 'Don't ask!'

'What happened?' Blanche laughed. 'Did you take a wrong turn and get lost on the mountain roads?'

'I almost wish I had. A car sideswiped me at that intersection at the bottom of the hill. The stupid man was speeding around the curve on my side of the road. He narrowly missed hitting me head-on. I was lucky to get away with a little dent on the front bumper.'

'You weren't hurt, were you?' watching anxiously as Tisha shook her head that she hadn't. 'That's a relief,' Blanche sighed. 'You haven't had a very good beginning on your first day here.'

'In every sunny day a little rain must fall,' Tisha quipped, determined not to think about her run in with Roarke Madison, but she couldn't shake that niggling feeling that she had come out second best in their exchange.

'I thought you might like the south bedroom. There's a great view from the window of the valley and our mountain.'

It was the middle of the afternoon before Tisha was

completely unpacked and had arranged her things in at least temporary order. She walked into the living-room and sank wearily into the smooth amber-covered cushions of the sofa. At almost the same instant her aunt appeared in the doorway of the kitchen carrying a tray of drinks and biscuits.

'All done?' she inquired. 'I was just coming in to suggest you take a break. How does iced tea and peanut butter cookies sound?'

'Heavenly!' Tisha replied, reaching for the frosted glass on the tray. 'Everything has been put somewhere, although I'm sure I'll change things around later.'

'Moving is always so hectic,' Blanche agreed as the front doorbell rang.

Tisha sipped at her drink as her aunt went to the door. The cool liquid was deliciously refreshing as it slipped down her throat. She rubbed the back of her neck, stretching her shoulders to ease the ache of her muscles from all the bending, stooping and lifting. The murmur of voices at the door registered only vaguely until she heard Blanche say in a cheery voice, 'Come on in. I want you to meet my niece.'

Then Tisha turned, curious to meet the visitor. The smile of greeting froze in her face as she stared at the man walking beside her aunt. His expression was coolly composed, while she felt as if the sofa had just been pulled from beneath her.

'You!' she gasped with disbelieving anger.

'Have you two met each other?' Blanche stared from

34

one to the other in confused surprise.

A smile ticked the corners of Roarke Madison's mouth. 'You might say we ran into each other before.'

'You ran into me,' Tisha corrected quickly.

'So I did,' he agreed, then turned to Blanche to explain, 'I was the one who put the dent in her bumper.'

'It was sheer luck that he didn't kill me,' Tisha retorted, sending him a malevolent glance.

'I see,' her aunt murmured, but her lips were compressed as though she were attempting to conceal a smile. 'In the circumstances, I don't know that introductions are in order.'

'I'd already guessed that she was your niece,' Roarke stated complacently, 'and I found out on my own that she's a provocative redhead.'

'My hair is auburn, for your information,' Tisha jeered. 'And I found out that you're not only a reckless driver, but an arrogantly conceited one, too!'

'Yes,' he smiled, not the least bit upset by her sarcasm. 'I believe you told me that earlier.'

'Roarke is also my neighbour,' Blanche inserted, her eyes twinkling at Tisha, carrying a message that she didn't understand at first. 'Remember? I said I wanted to introduce you to him.'

With sickening swiftness, Tisha remembered. He was the man her aunt had laughingly suggested she have an affair with. Vivid colour flowed into her cheeks and she was temporarily bereft of any reply. Worse, she felt his gaze studying her face with amused speculation.

'While I was in town, I arranged for you to have your car taken in tomorrow for the necessary repairs,' Roarke informed her, moving leisurely to take a chair opposite Tisha.

'Then you can cancel it,' she answered coldly. 'I told you I would make my own arrangements.'

'Don't be silly, Tisha,' Blanche intervened. 'It's terribly difficult to get a responsible person to work on your car. If Roarke has managed to get you an appointment, you would be wise to keep it.'

Tisha shot a fiery glance at the man, expecting to hear his hearty endorsement of her aunt's words, but he remained silent. How much easier it would have been to let her temper fly if he had attempted to persuade her to agree.

'I seem to have no choice,' she grumbled ungraciously.

To her surprise, he didn't seize on her submission with typical male superiority. Instead he gave her the name and the address of the repair shop with the air of a man who had carried out his responsibilities and had no more interest in the matter. Pursuing the subject would only make her look as if she was attempting some petty vengeance.

'If you're going into town tomorrow, I think I will too,' Blanche declared, setting her glass on a coaster. 'It's been weeks since I've had a thermal bath and massage. I'd better call now to make an appointment. What about you, Tish? The spas here are quite good and the thermal baths are extraordinarily stimulating. Shall I make an appointment for you?'

Her head moved in polite refusal. 'Another time.'

'While I'm on the phone, why don't you get Roarke a glass of iced tea?' her aunt suggested, moving lithely towards the studio and the telephone.

Tisha was quite willing to escape the glittering brightness of his brown eyes and the masculine presence that permeated the room with nearly physical reality. But the sound of unhurried footsteps behind her indicated her lack of success. She felt rather than saw him pause in the doorway, his lanky build filling the frame. The kitchen was totally foreign to her. She had opened three cupboard doors without finding the one that contained the glasses.

'I'll get it,' Roarke spoke from behind her, walking immediately to the correct cupboard.

'You know your way around very well, don't you?' Tisha jeered, watching as he unhesitatingly removed the pitcher of tea from the refrigerator and the ice cubes from the receptacle in the freezer.

His gaze slid over her, mocking yet seeming to physically touch her. 'Fairly well.'

'Do you come here often?' She deliberately put as much icy contempt in her voice as she could.

'What do you really want to know? Whether your aunt and I are or have been lovers?' His candour caught her by surprise. The thought had not consciously crossed her mind. 'Blanche is an attractive and warm woman.'

'She's at least ten years older than you!' The olive

37

green colour of her eyes deepened as horrified outrage widened their gaze.

'Considering the type of man you believe me to be, that shouldn't surprise you.'

'It doesn't surprise me. It disgusts me!' Tisha retorted sharply.

'Blanche tells me you've had a very strict upbringing. I imagine your outlook is very puritan on the male-female relationship.' The blond head was tilted in a patronizing gesture towards her rigid stance.

'She had no right to be talking about me to you!' The amused way he was looking at her made Tisha feel like an inexperienced teenager. 'I'm not exactly ignorant when it comes to sex and sexual relationships.'

'You have first-hand knowledge on the subject, do you?' One side of his mouth lifted in a doubting smile.

'That is strictly my business! Unlike a man, a woman doesn't go around bragging about her experiences with the opposite sex!' hiding from the cutting truth of his doubt with a burst of bravado.

There was a satanic gleam in his eyes as he made an insolent and leisurely inspection of her lithe form, pausing for an insulting moment on the quick rise and fall of her breasts beneath her white blouse now deprived of the protection of her jacket, before his gaze continued over her waist, the gentle swell of her hips and down her long slender legs.

'That's strange,' he murmured, his eyes returning with a knowing glitter to the heightened colour of her face. 'You don't have the look of a woman who's known a man. Maybe I'll have to reassess my opinion of you.'

'Don't bother!' Tisha ground out harshly.

'It's no bother. I've always liked challenges.' His tongue was very definitely in cheek as he met her murderous glance.

'Have you?' she asked sweetly. 'How's this for a challenge? I despise you!'

'That'll do for a start.' Roarke smiled, flashing a set of white teeth that contrasted sharply with the teak tan of his face. 'It might have been more interesting if you'd hated me, though.'

'I hate you, too!' Tisha declared, infuriated by the elephant toughness that warded off her poison darts. 'And you can save your interest for someone who appreciates it, like Blanche.'

'Blanche and I are friends. Nothing more,' he shrugged complacently.

'Really?' Tisha murmured sarcastically. 'That isn't the impression you gave me a moment ago.'

'I told you what you wanted to hear.'

He was looking at her in a way that made her blood pressure rise. She deliberately ignored the ring of truth in his voice, too filled with a frustrated anger at the way he had purposely tricked her.

'I see,' drawing the words through tightly clenched teeth. 'And it's through your friendship—' she paused, so her sneering emphasis on the last word could sink in, 'that you've acquired such an intimate knowledge of her house.'

'The truth is much more plausible than that.' He was actually grinning at her now. 'I designed it.'

Tisha felt as though she had just been impaled on a shaft of cold steel. 'What do you mean?'

'I'm an architect. I not only drew up the blueprint, but I also supervised its construction.'

'I didn't know,' she faltered.

'You didn't ask. You assumed.' A brown eyebrow lifted mockingly. 'I think you preferred to believe the worst possible reason for my knowledge of the house. It was more in keeping with your opinion of me.'

'You only wanted to make a fool of me,' Tisha accused, her anger surging to the foreground again.

'There's an over-used cliché that fits the situation. In your case, though, it's particularly apt. You're very beautiful when you're angry.' He straightened negligently away from the support of the counter. 'I guess I couldn't resist striking the match that would set you on fire.'

Blanche appeared in the kitchen doorway before the seething Tisha could think of a suitably cutting retort. 'What are you two talking about?' Her gaze shifted from the indifferent satisfaction on Roarke Madison's face to Tisha's smouldering rage. 'Is it a private war, or can anyone take part?'

'We were just discussing all the broken hearts Miss Caldwell had left behind,' Roarke answered.

His calm statement drew a puzzled frown. There had been absolutely no discussion regarding the romantic aspects of her life. 'I left no broken hearts,' she found herself saying, confused that he should even infer such a thing.

'I doubt that Kevin was overjoyed at your leaving,' Blanche reminded her.

'How did you manage to get rid of your fiancé?' Roarke inquired. The taunting glint in his dark eyes laughed at her astounded look as he let her know how thoroughly her aunt had discussed her niece with him.

'I simply explained that I wasn't the marrying kind and if I was, I wouldn't choose him,' Tisha answered bluntly. The truth was that she had been very apologetic when she had seen Kevin last. In spite of the callous declarations she had made to her father, she had tried to be as gently firm with Kevin as she could.

'Not very tactful, but I imagine he got the point,' Blanche laughed easily.

'So you have decided that marriage isn't for you.' Roarke ignored her reference to Kevin to pursue the first statement.

'I imagine that's about the only view you and I have in common,' she murmured with arch sweetness. 'Or am I wrong in presuming that you're a confirmed bachelor?'

'Oh, I'm a bachelor,' he assured her with laughter lurking in his voice. 'I can't exactly admit to being a confirmed one, though.'

'This looks as if it's going to be an interesting conversation.' Blanche's eyes twinkled brightly as she looked from one to the other. 'Let's go back into the living-room where I can relax and enjoy the fireworks.'

Tisha spun angrily on her heel to stalk out of the kitchen, but her destination was her own bedroom. She wanted no more conversation with the arrogantly cocky Roarke Madison. But she hadn't counted on his long, easy strides overtaking her before she reached the kitchen door, nor the hand that positively claimed her arm. Her skin tingled beneath his touch, sending liquid tongues of fire racing through her blood. She marked it off to the antagonism he aroused in her.

His low, silky voice murmured a message for her ears alone. 'Are you retreating before the battle has begun?'

Scorn was in the look Tisha gave him as she shook off his hand and marched into the living room. So he thought she was giving up without a fight, did he?

There was a look of false apology on her face when she turned it back to his carved features. 'It was foolish of me to refer to you as a confirmed bachelor. There's no such thing.'

'How did you come to that conclusion?' An indulgent light flashed into his eyes as he settled in the same chair as before.

'Well, no man is immune to the power of a woman if she chooses to wield it,' Tisha declared with an expressive movement of her shoulders. 'The Bible is full of such stories – Samson and Delilah, David and Bathsheba, Esther and King Ahasuerus. A woman always brings a man to his knees.' A smug smile pulled at the corners of her mouth as she stared into the brown eyes that held such mockery of her words in their depths. 'Don't you agree, Mr. Madison?'

There was a slight narrowing of his gaze as he refused to be trapped into any admission. 'Please go on. Your viewpoint is very enlightening.'

'Surely what I'm saying is obvious. When a man proposes, he's the one who gets down on his knees, not the other way around.' Her voice was the complacent purr of a cat toying with a mouse. Tisha noticed the surreptitious glance Blanche gave Roarke before she hid her smile behind the iced tea glass.

'That is a gesture of respect,' Roarke replied, 'but we men never do bow our heads.'

'We let you keep a little of your pride,' Tisha smiled sweetly. 'After all, if we wanted complete subservience, we'd buy a pet.'

'That's generous of you,' he chuckled. 'It's amazing how you've managed to convince yourself that you're doing a man a favour by marrying him when actually the benefits are all on the man's side.'

'How do you figure that?' Cold sarcasm dripped from her voice.

'For the price of food, clothing, shelter, and some pocket-money, a man gets a housekeeper, a laundrymaid, a cook, a seamstress, a dishwasher, a mother of his children, a babysitter, a nurse, an errand runner, and a bed partner. The wife also becomes a tax deduction. There are many advantages to marriage,' he concluded with a pseudo-serious expression.

'Of all the—!' Tisha sputtered, unable to put her frustration into words.

'I believe in looking at things logically and realistically,' Roarke smiled blandly. 'You can't deny that those are facts.'

'You're impossible!' she raged, rising to her feet to glare at him with impotent anger.

'You started this discussion,' he shrugged, the lines deepening around his mouth. 'If you don't like the heat, get away from the fire.'

'Gladly!' Tisha declared, and stalked out of the room.

CHAPTER THREE

'WHAT do you know about this Roarke Madison?'
Tisha asked sharply, taking her eyes from the road long
enough to glance at Blanche. 'I imagine he thinks he's
a lady-killer.'

'So you're interested in my neighbour,' the woman's
teasing voice answered. 'After the way you stalked
out of the room yesterday and then refused to let his
name enter any conversation, I was beginning to
wonder.'

'I'm not interested in him the way you mean.'
Tisha's fingers tightened on the wheel of the car, wishing it were his throat. 'It's simply intelligent to find out
all you can about a potential enemy.'

'You've formed an entirely wrong impression about
Roarke. He's not the domineering womaniser you
portray, if you'll excuse the use of an old-fashioned
noun,' Blanche stated. 'He's the most kind and con-
siderate neighbour I've ever known as well as a very
talented architect. I'll grant you with his looks and
relative wealth, there are any number of women
anxious for his company, but I've never pried in his
personal life nor he in mine.'

'And how do you explain his disgusting statement
about wives?' Tisha demanded angrily.

'You did rather invite that, you know. I thought he

took your slanderous digs at the male sex with considerable good-nature. There was a certain amount of truth in both your observations.'

'He's just like all men – he wants to keep women at home and in the kitchen.' A disgusted sigh followed her words as she made the turn on to the highway.

'Don't be downgrading the role of a woman as wife and mother,' Blanche scolded gently. 'There's nothing more challenging and rewarding than that. A great many women wouldn't be content in any other role.'

'I can't believe that you, of all women, should say such a thing!' Tisha declared, her voice sharpening in surprise.

'What do you mean? Me of all women?' her aunt inquired with a half-laugh.

'Well, you've never married. You have a successful career that you made on your own. You're an example for any liberated woman.'

'Do you know why I never married, Tish?' asked Blanche suddenly.

'I suppose because you never felt the need or desire to,' Tisha shrugged.

'There were a couple of times when I considered it very seriously.' Blanche levelly met her niece's curious look. 'But I was intelligent enough to realize that I was basically a very selfish person. I didn't want the responsibility that a husband and family would mean. In a sense I was not only selfish but a coward as well. I don't regret my decision and, given the chance, I wouldn't change it. You see, Tisha, it's an individual thing that has nothing to do with being a man or a woman.'

'What are you saying? That you're the exception to prove the rule?' Tisha's voice held none of the sharpness and cynicism of earlier as she spoke in a quietly serious tone.

'I'm saying that few people can make that kind of commitment to their career.'

'Can I?'

'Do you live to paint?' Blanche asked softly, a burning light creeping into her eyes. 'Is art the ultimate goal?'

The ultimate goal? Tisha didn't think she knew what her ultimate goal was. She had not the unique talent of her aunt, a fact she recognized. Without that, she wouldn't find the fulfilment that Blanche knew.

She answered her aunt's question hesitantly but truthfully. 'Painting is a hobby for me that I try to earn my living by.'

'And it's a hobby that combines very well with married life.'

'Now you sound like my father,' Tisha accused, softening her words with a smile. 'Trying to marry me off for my own good.'

'Only to the man you love.'

'If there is such a creature.' Her laughter added the exclamation point. 'It would be terrible if all I met were the Roarke Madisons of this world.'

'I wouldn't eliminate Roarke as husband material. I'm certain your failure to fall at his feet has piqued his interest, and you aren't indifferent to him either.'

Tisha wrinkled her nose in distaste. 'He brings out the worst in me.'

'Maybe it's a defence mechanism to keep from being attracted to him,' her aunt chided.

'I don't want a man who thinks he's going to be the lord and master over my life!' The defiant tilt of her chin accented the swan-like column of her throat.

'You wouldn't be happy with someone you could walk over either. A little mastery wouldn't be too bad as long as the iron hand was gloved in velvet.'

'Blanche, you're as stubborn as my father.' There was a resigned shake of her head in the direction of the white lock streaking her aunt's hair. 'Are you really trying to pair me off with him?'

'He's my neighbour. I wouldn't exactly like you to declare war on him. It would be much more peaceful if the two of you were friends,' Blanche suggested with a twinkle in her eye.

'I'll agree to this much,' Tisha compromised, 'I won't pick a fight with him.'

'That's a beginning,' Blanche smiled, glancing out the windows at the cluster of buildings. 'You can let me out at this corner. Bath House Row is only a block away.'

After dropping her aunt at the corner, Tisha continued through the business district to the repair shop. As she pulled into the drive, the first car she saw was the white sports car belonging to Roarke Madison. Her lips compressed into a tight line as she parked her own car and walked into the office.

'Right on time,' Roarke murmured, straightening from his leaning position against a side wall.

'What are you doing here?' Tisha demanded, forgetting completely her earlier promise that she would not antagonize this man.

'The damage wasn't only to your car,' he chided with that hint of laughter in his eyes. 'Among other things, I put out a headlight. They've just finished with mine.'

'I see,' she said grimly, wondering why she had thought he was there to see her. A man in greasy overalls walked into the room and she turned her attention to him.

'Hi, Mac,' Roarke greeted him. 'This is Miss Caldwell.'

The man's gaze slid admiringly over Tisha before it twinkled back to Roarke. 'Now I understand why you ran into her. You have some unusual ways of meeting new girls.'

A rush of anger coloured her cheeks, but she quickly subdued it. 'Here are the keys to my car. It's the blue Mustang.'

'It'll be ready in a couple of hours,' the man named Mac replied as he accepted the keys, misinterpreting the glitter in her green eyes when she glanced at Roarke. When he turned to leave, Tisha heard the muttered aside he directed at Roarke. 'You sure know how to pick them. She's better than the one before and younger, too.'

'Are your conquests always such common knowledge?' Tisha hissed the instant they were alone.

'Do you classify yourself as one of my conquests?' a lock of sun-bleached hair waved rakishly near his forehead as he tilted his head mockingly towards her.

'I'm glad to say that I don't have that dishonour!'

A coaxing smile appeared on his face. 'Would you have preferred that I told the man that we didn't get along? He wouldn't have believed me. What difference does it make what he thinks?'

It shouldn't have made any difference, Tisha admitted to herself as she recognized the logic in his words. 'I didn't care for the way he made it sound as if we'd gone to bed together.'

She noticed that whenever he attempted to hide a smile, the cleft in his chin became more noticeable.

'You profess to be a liberated woman, yet your morals are decidedly old-fashioned,' he mocked.

'At least I can't be accused of being promiscuous,' she said with saccharine sweetness. 'Unlike you, I don't hop into bed with every man I meet.'

'Neither do I,' he murmured lazily.

'Don't you?' A finely drawn brow arched doubtingly in his direction.

There was a seductive quality in the way his eyes moved over her face. Her heart skipped a beat at the almost physical caress.

'I haven't been to bed with you,' Roarke drawled, adding softly and with deliberate provocation, 'yet.'

'Oooh!' Tisha's foot stamped the floor in anger

before she pivoted around and marched out the door.

But those lithe, superior strides caught up with her in seconds and a hand closed over her arm, jerking her to a halt. 'Where are you going?' his laughing voice asked her.

'Anywhere away from you!' she retorted, her head thrown back to look with malevolent dislike into his ruggedly handsome face.

'I was striking matches again. I apologize.' The force of his virilely masculine charm was focused directly on her.

Her breathing was coming in uneven spurts. 'Your apology is not accepted,' Tisha declared, trying to twist her arm free of his hold gracefully. 'Now, let me go!'

'I promise not to bait you any more,' he coaxed, seemingly oblivious to her efforts to get loose as he held her easily.

'You irritate me just by breathing!' she hissed.

'Well, I'm not going to die to prove that I'm sorry,' Roarke smiled. 'Let's call a truce. After all, we are on neutral ground.'

'Are we? I hadn't realized any ground beneath your feet could be classified as neutral!' Her eyes flashed up at him before she turned her head away, her toes tapping out a war-beat on the pavement.

'How did you intend to pass the time waiting for your car?' he asked.

'I certainly don't intend to spend it with you!' Tisha declared, refusing to succumb to the persuasive sound of his voice. 'I'm going to do some sketching. Now will you please let go of my arm?'

His head moved downward in an acknowledging nod. 'That's right, you're an artist, aren't you, like your aunt.'

'Hardly like Blanche,' she corrected automatically. 'She's an artist. I dabble in art.'

'And I thought I was in the company of a budding genius. You do have the temperament of one,' Roarke mocked.

'You can't accuse my aunt of having an artistic temperament. A more good-natured person you're unlikely to meet. So don't pin that label on me.'

'Blanche had to be as independent as you are or she wouldn't have succeeded on her own. By the same token, she's a warm and sensitive woman, undoubtedly the side she shows to her family.'

'That's the way it should be.' Too late Tisha remembered her promise not to argue with this man, but she tried to reconcile herself with the fact that he had deliberately provoked her, which was not wholly true.

'To get back to my original question, where are you going to do your sketching?'

'I thought I'd catch a taxi or bus downtown,' she replied in a less abrasive tone.

'Get your sketch pad and whatever else you need and I'll give you a ride,' he ordered, a bland smile on his face.

Tisha prickled at the way he expected her to obey. 'If I accept your offer, will you leave me alone then?'

'I'll consider it,' his brown eyes twinkled as he released her arm.

'In that much hoped-for event, I'll agree to let you drive me there,' Tisha gave in.

'Careful!' his mocking voice called after her as she started to walk to her car, 'or you might sound too eager for my company.'

'That'll be the day!' she shot back with a bitter laugh.

Minutes later Tisha was inside his car, hugging herself close to the door to keep as much distance between them as was possible. But Roarke seemed to pay no notice as he pulled out into the sparse traffic on the street.

'Do you know much about Hot Springs?' he questioned.

'I've been here before,' Tisha shrugged, sweeping a strand of her hair over her shoulder in a gesture of indifference.

'Which doesn't mean anything,' he concluded. 'You've lived in Little Rock all your life, haven't you?'

'Yes,' she replied, clipping off the end of the word with her teeth.

'And like most people you never bothered to explore what was in your own back yard, am I right?' He darted her a knowing look.

'If you mean that when Father and I took our vacations, did we come here, then the answer is no,' Tisha snapped. 'We usually went west or south.'

'Then you actually know very little about Hot Springs?' Roarke persisted.

'It has hot springs,' she commented sarcastically. A quick glance out the window took in Arlington Park which signalled the beginning of Bath House Row. 'You can let me out here.'

Instead of pulling up at the corner, Roarke manoeuvred his car into a parking space. Before Tisha could gather her things and escape, he was out of the car, had put coins in the meter, and was at her elbow.

'Thank you for the lift, Mr. Madison.' She knew even as she said the words that she couldn't dismiss him so easily.

He looked down at her, mischief gleaming in his dark eyes. 'I wouldn't be doing my duty as a resident if I didn't impart a little of the city's illustrious history to you.'

Through gritted teeth, she said, 'You just won't take "no" for an answer, will you?'

He gave her a lazy glance and smiled. 'I don't believe you would think very much of me if I did.'

For a moment Tisha was startled by his answer. She had the odd feeling that what he said was true. Blanche had said that Tisha wouldn't respect a man she could walk over. Yet, paradoxically, she resented being dominated. It was the last thought that roused her from her silence.

'I don't like things shoved down my throat because someone else thinks they're good for me,' she said coldly.

'Does anyone?' Roarke murmured. The light flashed to WALK and he ushered her unceremoniously across

54

the street. 'Of course, the redeeming side to that is that sometimes it's the only way we find out if we like something.'

Tisha studied the strength in his jawline, the chiselled cheekbones and nose, passed over the faint cleft in his jutting chin, hesitated a second on the sensual line of his mouth before lifting her gaze to his eyes.

'You still can't let yourself agree with me, can you?' Roarke said softly, but he didn't wait for her to reply. 'The Indians called this place the Valley of the Vapours. This ground was sacred to all tribes. They came here in peace to bathe their sick and wounded in the springs. I mentioned earlier that we were on neutral ground. I'm willing to declare a temporary truce if you are.'

It was an offer of compromise that wasn't really a compromise, but there was a humorous lift to her mouth. 'What a choice!' Tisha murmured. 'If I don't willingly agree to have you guide me around, you're going to do it anyway.'

'It is somewhat of a Hobson's choice, isn't it?' Roarke chuckled complacently. For the first time since they had met, her answering smile was one of genuine amusement and it brought a sparkling glitter to her eyes, which caused an unreadable expression to creep into the dark gaze that dwelt on her face.

'Pass the peacepipe, then,' she sighed.

'Since I don't have one, will a handshake do?'

The firm pressure of the large hand closing over hers sent a pleasant rush of warmth through her bloodstream. And the sensation remained even after he released her hand. A slow, captivating smile spread over his face. Its dazzling brilliance almost blinded her as she turned in answer to the guiding pressure of his hand on her back.

'We'll walk along the promenade first,' Roarke announced in a low, musically pitched tone that seemed to vibrate around her. 'It will better set the mood for the early history.'

He had shortened his supple, athletic strides to match hers as they walked the paved pathway towards the tree-covered mountain rising in the heart of the city.

'You must tell me everything about Hot Springs,' Tisha commanded in a playful taunt.

'All the Indians knew about the springs and their stories of its restorative powers were passed from tribe to tribe,' Roarke began with mocking compliance. 'It's believed that these tales sent Ponce de Leon on his search for the Fountain of Youth, but unfortunately he never travelled far enough inland to find it. Therefore the first European to view the steaming valley of the vapours was the Spanish gold-seeker Hernando DeSoto, guided here by friendly Indians.' A huge rock blocked their path and Tisha stopped when Roarke did. 'The plaque on this tufa rock commemorates DeSoto's arrival here in 1541.'

Then he led her around the rock to the steps leading up the hillside to a wide, tree-sheltered brick walk scattered with benches and tables.

'But it was La Salle who came here in 1682,' he went

on, 'and claimed the territory for France. If you remember your American history, the territory was given to Spain, then returned to France again in the secret treaty of Madrid in 1801. Subsequently Napoleon sold it to the United States as part of the Louisiana Purchase. President Jefferson, who initiated the purchase, sent two scientists here the following year to find out more about the hot water that flowed from the mountain.'

'You said it was called the Valley of the Vapours. Why aren't there any vapours now?'

'That's because of the forty-seven springs only two have been left open for display purposes. The rest have been channelled into an underground reservoir where they're piped into the various bath houses,' he explained. 'The City of Hot Springs is set in the middle of a national park. An Act of Congress in 1832 set aside the entire area, but later amended it to allow the town to grow about it.' His hand moved to her elbow to guide her towards a set of steps. 'The display springs are below us.'

Back against the side of the mountain were two clear pools of steaming water set amongst rocks much like the large one Tisha had seen at the beginning of their walk. It was a very peaceful, sylvan setting, a miniature glade behind the row of commercial bathhouses. Her fingers dipped quickly in and out of the hot water pool.

'The temperature of the water averages a hundred and forty-three degrees Fahrenheit as it flows out of the mountain,' Roarke smiled.

'What makes it so hot?'

'There are several theories about that, none of which have been proved. All the thermal water from the hot springs naturally possess radium emanation, which is believed to be the cause of the heat.'

'It is rather fascinating, isn't it?'

'I'm glad you're not too stubborn to admit it,' he commented, looking into the tranquil depths of her seagreen eyes.

An expression of chagrin chased across her face before Tisha inquired quickly in an effort to change the subject, 'Is there more?'

'The history of Hot Springs would fill a book. All I did was give you the general highlights. This was the temporary headquarters of the State Government during the Civil War. The city was the termination point of the legendary Diamond Jo railroad. We'll skip the part that this was a favourite resort of the notorious Al Capone.' He stretched out his hand towards her. 'Come on, let's walk some more.'

Tisha didn't think twice about accepting his hand, nor leaving it there as they retraced their way back up the steps to the quiet mountainside promenade. A squirrel scampered along the brick railing beside them, stopping every now and then to sit on his haunches and chatter at them.

'I think he's doing a bit of begging,' Roarke chuckled. 'The small animals around here are quite tame.'

'Next time I'll remember to bring something,' Tisha

promised the persistent squirrel.

He followed them for several more yards before he finally decided there would be no handout and raced back the way he had come. The pair continued past two older gentlemen seated at a concrete table, engrossed in a game of checkers.

'Would you like to sit down for a while?' Roarke asked, motioning towards a bench on the side of the walk near the mountain.

Tisha slid on to the bench in silent acceptance, placing her bag and sketch pad on the table. She felt sublimely content. The traffic on the street beyond and below them was muffled by the lush foliage of the trees beginning their transformation from their summer dress to their autumn cloaks. She watched with idle indifference as Roarke reached behind them to pluck a late blooming dandelion and twirl it in his fingers. Then his dark gaze moved over to her face to study it with silent thoroughness.

'I wonder if you like men?' he mused.

A tiny creasing frown knitted her forehead as she tried to follow his thoughts. One corner of his mouth lifted in a smile as he noticed her confusion.

'I think we'd better find out,' Roarke murmured, reaching out with one hand to tilt her chin while he held the yellow dandelion beneath it. The clear skin of her throat reflected the luminous amber colour of the wild flower. 'Umm, that was a very positive reaction!'

There was no coyness in the glinting laughter in her eyes as she met his gaze and remembered this game she had played as a child.

'What about you?' she teased easily, her hand covering his to move it under his chin. Roarke allowed the initial movement then, stiffening his arm before the dandelion reached its destination.

'It won't work on men over thirty,' he smiled, and Tisha became suddenly conscious of how close his face was to hers, and the disturbing way his gaze was resting on her mouth. 'Too much beard!'

She fought off the attack of breathlessness as she removed her hand from the warmth of his and put a safe distance between them. 'It's all right,' she declared airily. 'I already know you find women very attractive.'

'And how do you know that?' he asked quietly, a trace of mockery in his smile.

Tisha shrugged, as if to say her sources were secret, but declined a verbal answer to his question. Instead she drew her foot on to the bench and wrapped her arms around her knee to study the less disturbing scenery.

'It's very peaceful here, isn't it?' she commented.

'You even manage to pretend you're enjoying my company,' Roarke jibed.

'I can force myself to be pleasant to anyone if the surroundings are sufficiently distracting.' She had become too physically aware of him and had resorted to stinging words to protect herself from further moments of vulnerability.

'Why did you revert back to a waspish tongue?' A quizzically amused frown appeared on the tanned forehead. 'Are you afraid of being a woman?'

'What nonsense! I already am a woman.' Her eyes widened at his question, a suggestion of hauteur in the tilt of her head.

'Prove it.' His dark eyes challenged. 'Have dinner with me Friday night.'

Tisha recoiled slightly. 'Why?'

'Why do you think?' he countered.

'I suppose your arrogant male pride,' her expression was deliberately coldly scornful, 'is suffering because you haven't been able to conquer me. I haven't fallen into your arms or your bed with the alacrity of the other women you've known. You probably think with wine and candlelight you'll be able to seduce me.'

'The thought does have a ring of appeal,' he admitted.

'Then we'll simply forget you made the invitation, Mr. Madison,' Tisha declared, reaching stiffly forward to gather her bag and sketch pad.

'Call me Roarke,' he instructed with infuriating calm. 'If we're going out Friday, we should be on first-name terms.'

A furrow of exasperation slashed across her brows as she glanced back at him. 'Didn't you hear what I said? I'm not going!'

'Why? After after all your fervent avowals that women are the superior sex, don't you think you're capable of parrying my advances?' he inquired with a satirical quirk of his brow. 'Or maybe you don't really believe all that nonsense you've been spouting?'

'Of course I do!' she cried angrily.

'Then why are you so afraid to go out with me?'

'I'm not!'

'Good. I'll pick you up at seven.' Roarke rose lazily to his feet and sketched her a mocking salute before walking away. Tisha's mouth was still working to find the proper words of protest even after he was out of hearing.

CHAPTER FOUR

FOR three days she tried to come up with plausible reasons to cancel her date with Roarke Madison. A half a dozen times, she reached for the telephone to call only to back away, knowing how he would poke holes in her weak excuses. Blanche was no help at all, believing Tish had accepted the date in an effort to make peace with her neighbour. Her aunt had been so delighted by her concession that Tisha had been left with no recourse except to go.

Roarke arrived precisely at seven o'clock, but Tisha was deliberately not ready. A half an hour later she walked into the living room knowing full well the olive and peacock blue caftan accented the colour of her eyes, sparkling now with the light of battle. It had taken nearly three-quarters of an hour just to coil her long hair on top of her head to shimmer in the artificial light like a mink crown. Only sunlight could turn it to fire. The style added years and an illusion of experience.

'I was beginning to think you were going to stand me up.' Roarke rose to his feet, impeccably dressed in dark evening clothes. Unhurried steps brought him to her side where he towered intimidatingly over her, dark eyes sweeping her in insolent appraisal.

'Now why would you think such a thing?' Tisha

asked sweetly.

His finger touched the jade stone hanging from her ear and sent it swinging. His voice was a husky murmur meant for her ears alone.

'Maybe it's that little pulse jumping in your throat that tells me you aren't quite as poised as you appear.' Louder he said for Blanche's benefit, 'We'd better be going.'

Tisha was forced to dim the angry light that had leapt into her eyes as she turned to bid her aunt goodnight. It was exceedingly difficult not to pull away from the hand that gripped her elbow.

'We won't be late, Blanche,' she promised, brushing the woman's cheek with her lips.

'You two enjoy yourselves.' Then with a wink at Tisha, she added in a teasing whisper, 'Remember, twenty minutes and the porchlight comes on!'

The flush on Tisha's cheeks wasn't caused by rouge as she darted a speaking glance at her escort. 'There won't be any need of that tonight.' She knew there would be no lingering goodnights taken outside the door.

'What was that about?' Roarke asked as, minutes later, he opened the car door for her.

'A family joke,' not meeting his glittering eyes as she made sure her long skirt was out of the way so he could close the door.

A golden sunset had painted the western sky with dusky amber and cream colours and Tisha pretended to be studying it when Roarke slipped behind the wheel.

'You don't think we're going to be reluctant to bid each other goodnight when the evening is over?' he queried, a brow lifting in mockery as she turned in surprise. 'I've had my share of porchlights turned on by impatient parents.'

'What? No shotguns?' she asked sarcastically.

'No, no shotguns.' With a flick of the wrist, he started the motor and reversed out of the drive.

Tisha folded her hands primly in her lap. 'I hope they'll hold our dinner reservation.'

'I took the precaution of making it for eight o'clock,' Roarke replied, a suppressed smile deepening the lines around his nose and mouth. 'In case you took your time in dressing.'

He seemed to thwart her at every turn, she thought angrily. 'You're probably more accustomed to women undressing for you, aren't you?'

'You could call it Madison's Law.' He was definitely laughing at her attempts to belittle him. 'What goes on must come off.'

'Well, you didn't see fit to tell me where we were going,' Tisha announced. 'It's difficult choosing what to wear when I didn't know if we were going to a hamburger joint or a steak house.'

'Obviously you realized I wasn't as impoverished as the boys you're accustomed to dating.' His glance slid over her sophisticated attire. 'I hope all that hair on top of your head doesn't give you a headache.'

'Only my escort is capable of that,' she retorted sharply. 'It won't make me top-heavy either. I'm not likely to stumble and embarrass you.'

'The thought never entered my mind.' His voice was as dry as the wind blowing off the Mojave Desert. 'But don't get any ideas about accidentally dumping your food or drink in my lap tonight or I'll be forced to drop mine on top of your pretty head.'

There was a steely quality to his voice that Tisha had never noticed before. It was that more than his warning that sat her back in her seat in silence for the rest of the drive. Roarke Madison was not only prepared to fence words with her, but he was also prepared to match fire with fire, and no holding back because she was a woman.

In the car-park of the restaurant, Tisha deliberately stepped out of the car before Roarke could walk around to open the door for her. His eyes narrowed fractionally when he saw her standing with a challenging tilt to her head. If he was decreeing that the gloves were off, then she was going to follow all the way through.

'I take it you don't want to observe the courteous acts a man does for a woman. So be it,' he declared. A street light gleamed on the bleached brown head that inclined mockingly towards her.

The swish of her long skirt had a regally haughty sound as Tisha swept ahead of him. Unfortunately the high heels of her shoes made speed impossible and Roarke was soon walking even with her, smiling at the disdainful expression on her face. As they reached the restaurant building, he moved ahead, opening the door and stepping through it, leaving Tisha to grope quickly for the handle before it slammed in her face. Her cheeks were flushed with anger when she caught up with him inside.

Brown eyes flicked over her briefly, but long enough for Tisha to receive his message – she had wanted it this way. Before she could make a cutting retort the maître d'hotel was leading them to their table.

They were barely seated when the cocktail waitress appeared. 'A dry Martini,' Roarke ordered, completely ignoring Tisha and forcing the waitress to ask her preference.

'A daiquiri,' she requested through gritted teeth.

The poison arrow in the look she slung at Roarke was deflected by the shield of his menu. Angrily she opened her own, her hands trembling so badly she could barely read the print. With a burst of temper, Tisha shoved her menu on the table.

'This is impossible!' she hissed as Roarke lowered his to glance at her with an elevated brow. 'You might as well take me home, because I'm not going to put up with this!'

She moved her chair away from the table and started to get up. 'Sit down,' he ordered, then repeated it in a more forceful tone. 'Sit down or I'll sit you down!'

And Tisha knew he was hateful enough to do just that Reluctantly she leaned back in her seat and watched with seething indignation the slow smile that spread over his tanned face without reaching the glittering brown eyes.

'You're despicable!' she murmured savagely. For all his relaxed air, she had the impression of a cougar, sleek and golden, waiting to pounce on his prey.

'If you don't want to act like a lady, I have no intention of being a gentleman,' Roarke replied. 'It's up to you whether we continue this war of insults or enjoy the evening.'

'It would be impossible to enjoy your domineering presence,' she spat.

His mouth tightened fractionally before he relaxed it into a mocking smile. 'Do you deny that our truce the other afternoon produced a pleasant result?'

The waitress arrived with their drinks, giving Tisha an opportunity to think about her answer before she replied. Her fingers closed around the fragile stem of the champagne-type glass as she made a pretence of studying it.

'I won't deny that the afternoon had its pleasant aspect,' she agreed, flashing him a defiant look that conflicted with the seeming compliance of her tone. 'As a tour guide you were informative and interesting. It was later when you attempted to win me with your charm that I found it intolerable to continue the truce.'

'If you felt that way, why did you agree to go out with me tonight?' Amusement glinted in the look he bestowed on her.

'I didn't agree,' Tisha reminded him bitterly. 'You tricked me into accepting.'

'Do you mean a mere man manoeuvred an intelligent female like you into going out with him?'

Her palm itched with a desire to slap that mockingly innocent look from his face.

'And I thought you were trying to convince me that men were all muscle with very little brain,' he concluded wryly. 'Maybe your opinion needs some revising.'

'I never meant to imply that men weren't cunning,' Tisha retorted.

'You have quite a vocabulary,' Roarke chuckled. 'And you always manage to pick the right word that will turn a compliment into an insult.'

'How perceptive of you to notice!' It was her finely drawn brow that arched mockingly in his direction.

'Shall we order now?' he inquired, picking up his menu again. 'You might like the flaming shish-kebab. It would match your temper.'

'What will you be having? The bass? It doesn't say whether it's large mouth or not.'

He ignored the dripping sweetness of her voice. 'As a matter of fact, I think I'll have the shish-kebab. It suits my taste.'

The meal was a disaster. Tisha ended up ordering a steak, but the succulently juicy cut of beef had no taste for her. She could have been chewing leather for all the notice she paid. Her only thought was to get the meal over with and return to her aunt's. She declined after-dinner coffee and then was forced to sit at the table while Roarke drank his.

'Are we ready to go now?' she demanded impatiently when he finally placed the empty cup in its saucer.

'I believe so,' he smiled, and signalled to the waiter for their bill.

There were more moments of waiting while the man returned with the change before Roarke rose from his chair. Tisha walked swiftly towards the exit door, eager to be gone, but his fingers closed over the soft flesh of her upper arm and slowed her down.

'There's a small dance floor on the other side of the restaurant area. I thought we'd spend an hour or two there.'

Her neck stiffened at his words as she glared up at him. 'And if I insist that you take me home?'

'Ah, but you won't, will you?' He looked down with arrogant sureness. 'You wouldn't want to deprive me of your vital company. Or should I have said volatile?'

'You should have said unwilling,' she answered sharply, but didn't resist when he turned her away from the door down the hallway to a dimly lit room.

The room was crowded with couples gathered around small tables illuminated by flickering amber candles. Tisha had difficulty adjusting her eyes to the relative darkness of the room and was forced to rely on Roarke's guidance as he led her to a small circular table. A combo was playing a selection of slow ballads from a raised platform in one corner of the room.

'Shall we dance?' Roarke asked after he had ordered their drinks.

Ill temper had stretched her nerves to the breaking

point as she sent him a glance of malevolent dislike. 'That's what we came here for, wasn't it?'

'I have a feeling you're going to walk all over my feet,' he murmured as they rose from the table together to traverse the short distance to the dance floor.

Tisha didn't tell him that he needn't worry on that score. She had no intention of being that close to him. The hand that closed over hers seemed unnaturally warm compared to the icy temperature of her fingers. Her other hand wasn't so much resting on his shoulder as pushing against it while his hand at the back of her waist firmly guided her into matching his steps. Tisha kept her gaze averted from the vicinity of his face.

His arm tightened around her waist. 'Relax,' he said softly. The hand holding hers tightened as he folded his arm around hers and drew it forcibly against the hardness of his chest. The action brought her closer to him while his iron grip held her there. Thankfully the music ended and Roarke was compelled to release her.

At their table, he seemed disinclined to continue the conversation as he leaned back in his chair to study Tisha in quiet contemplation. She took a tentative sip of the drink she didn't want, then replaced it on its coaster. The small band was playing an upbeat tune. She tried to enjoy it, but she found the growing silence of her escort was too disturbing.

Tearing her swizzle stick apart. she glanced into the shadows that hid his face. 'You can't want to dance with me again.' she declared, 'so why don't we leave?'

'I think we should stay.'

71

'Why?' Exasperation blew out the angry, sighing question. 'We surely aren't going to sit at this table and stare at each other?'

The band had switched again to a slower ballad and Roarke was standing beside her chair, pulling her to her feet. The arm around her waist kept her at his side until they reached the dance floor. He turned her into his arms so quickly that she didn't realize what was happening until she discovered both his hands were linked together in the small of her back, moulding her hips against his muscular thighs. Her own hands were ineffectually pressed against his chest to hold some part of her body away from him. There was no mistaking the glare of hostility in her eyes as she looked at the complacent smile on his face.

Tisha's fingers doubled into tight fists as she fought the impulse to beat at his chest in an effort to be free. She lowered her head, staring at the whiteness of his shirt, determined to endure the embrace without making a scene. The spread of his fingers on her spine burned through the jersey material of her caftan. A liquid fire shot through her limbs as she felt their movement over her hips in a guiding caress while Roarke moulded her against the hardness of his body.

The exploring caress of his hands became a bit too daring and Tisha could not stop herself from whispering angrily, 'Stop it!'

At the same time, she reached down to put his hands back on her waist. Instantly she realized her mistake. Without the leverage of her hands against his chest, he completed the embrace with one hand between her shoulders bringing her against his chest.

'I don't like to dance this way,' she told his collar while her fingers dug into the expensive material of his jacket sleeves.

'Why ever not?' he asked, nuzzling her ear.

'It's my old-fashioned morals again,' she muttered sarcastically. 'I don't like embracing in public.'

There was no escaping his touch. She felt every muscle contraction in his body and a growing weakness attacked her legs.

'Don't be embarrassed,' Roarke murmured. 'Nobody is watching us.'

The warmth of his breath played along her neck. 'I don't care!' She tilted her head back to stop the trail of fire along her neck and to let the glitter of her anger be directed to his carved face.

'Are you afraid of an unexpected kiss?' he taunted her. His lazy, half-closed eyes were focused on her lips.

'There's no such thing. A girl always expects to be kissed. It's only the where and the when she doesn't know,' Tisha answered.

'We must answer those two questions, then.' Warmly and briefly his mouth touched hers, then he was once again looking down at her, watching the hot colour steal over her cheeks.

'Was that the best you could do?' she asked, surprised to find her breathing was shallow and uneven.

The glinting humour in his eyes took in the other dancers around them. 'In the circumstances,' he answered smoothly.

'I didn't realize discretion was one of your virtues,' she taunted.

'I didn't know you thought I had any virtues,' he returned, the quirking eyebrow laughing at her again.

The instant the song ended, Tisha wrenched herself free of his unresisting arms. She had just seated herself in her chair when Roarke arrived at their table. Instead of sitting down, he stood beside her chair and touched her shoulder, smiling when she shrank away.

'I thought you wanted to leave,' he mocked.

Tisha sent him another furious glance as she rose to her feet. She closed her mouth on the cutting comment that hovered on the tip of her tongue. She didn't want to take any chances that he might change his mind.

The moon was a silver cartwheel in the velvet dark sky sprinkled with silver stars winking down at her as she stared out the car window, determined to ignore the man behind the wheel. Her skin still seemed to tingle with the sensual remembrance – of her body pressed against his. It was a disquieting sensation.

'Am I to receive the silent treatment now?' Roarke asked. 'It's hard to believe that you've run out of insults.'

'Spare me your sarcasm,' she answered in a tightly controlled voice. 'I'm tired. All I want to do is get home.'

'It's been an enervating evening,' he agreed.

'Marked by highlights of boredom,' she could not

resist inserting.

A low chuckle sounded from his side of the car. 'There, for a minute, I thought your defences were down.'

'You can think again!' she retorted.

'You'll fight me with your last breath, won't you?' he murmured softly.

'You won't last that long.'

Tall pines on either side of the country road blocked out the moonlight. Tisha watched the car headlights pick out the turn that led to Blanche's.

'As the song says, when an irresistible object meets up with an immovable one, something has to give,' Roarke chuckled again.

'I suppose you classify yourself as an irresistible object,' she hooted with thick sarcasm. 'I have news for you, Mr. Madison, the strong, masterful type turns my stomach.'

'Blanche tells me that your father is a forceful, independent man. Is that true?' he asked, making an abrupt change in subject.

'Yes, I take after him in that respect. I'm not influenced by outward glitter and charm.' Tisha gave him a scathing look that was useless in the dim interior of the car.

'I've heard it said that girls tend to marry men who resemble their fathers,' Roarke jibed.

Her muscles tensed as a quiver of apprehension attacked her. She had heard that theory before. As a child and teenager she had subscribed to it, thinking there could be nothing more wonderful than to marry a man as masculine and unconquerable as her father. Of course that was before she had to live under his tyranny of the last few years.

'In some cases it might be true, but not in mine,' she averred.

'Why?'

'Because the man I marry has to respect me as an individual and not regard me as his chattel to be ordered and dictated to as if I didn't have any sense of my own. He'll not only have to love me, but he'll have to trust me too and not ... not ...' Her hand waved through the air as she searched for the right word to complete her thought.

'And not turn on porchlights,' Roarke supplied.

'Yes,' she nodded sharply, her hand returning to her lap, 'in the sense that he shouldn't feel the need to check up on me.'

'Is that the way your father treated your mother?'

Tisha sat very still. Of all the arguments between her parents, there had not been one born of jealousy or mistrust that she could remember. Their love for each other had been very strong and displayed in many ways.

'No, he never doubted her,' she answered quietly.

'Your mother must have been a very passive woman.'

'My mother?' Tisha laughed. 'She was every bit as stubborn as Dad. They argued a lot, never with any bitterness or vindictiveness, though. I remember they would be in the middle of some heated debate and one or the other would burst into laughter and it would be all over. They had a one-in-a-million marriage.'

'When did you lose your mother?'

'When I was fourteen.'

'Your father must have taken it very hard.'

'He did. He wandered around the house like a lost soul for a long time,' Tisha admitted. 'Dad and I were very close those first years after Mom died. But these last three years,' she shuddered, remembering some of their more voluble quarrels, 'he's been impossible to live with'.

'Daddy's little girl grew up on him, and very beautifully, too,' Roarke commented. 'Being a man who's tasted the wild fruits, your father knows how easily a man can take advantage of an attractive girl like you. No doubt that's why he wants to get you married and out of temptation's path.'

His compliment and the subsequent suggestive statement pulled Tisha sharply out of her reverie of the past. A light in the window of her aunt's home beamed a welcome to her as she realized they were parked in the drive. She chided herself severely for dropping her guard even for a minute. She had no wish for Roarke to know anything about her past life.

'You can be certain my father would never have let me go out with a wolf like you,' she declared, her hand reaching for the door handle.

His movement was quicker and surer as his fingers closed over her wrist before she could achieve her objective. 'Not so fast!' His dark face was very close to hers, causing Tisha to draw back against her seat. 'No self-respecting wolf would let a lovely woman like you get away without a goodnight kiss.'

There was a drumbeat in her ears that she finally recognized as the pounding of her blood. 'I should have known you were one of those disgusting males who expect payment for taking a girl out,' she snapped, but her mouth felt unusually dry.

'That's right,' he agreed smoothly.

His hand closed over her chin, lifting it to receive his kiss. It was deep and lingering, confirming her assertion that he had known a lot of women. Yet the lack of force in the tantalizing caress made it all the more potent and difficult to resist. When his mouth finally left hers, Tisha felt he had burned his brand into the softness of her lips. She exhaled a quivering breath, relaxing the control that had held her stiffly resistant under his touch.

'Now may I go?' surprised that she was still able to put so much freezing scorn in her voice.

His face was still close enough for her to see the deep smiling grooves around his mouth. In answer, he reached down and pulled the handle, opening the door. The interior light flicked on, glimmering on the golden lights in his hair while Tisha slipped out of her seat and quickly slammed the door.

Billy Goat Gruff was between her and the door, but she scurried past. It wasn't the goat watching her that made her legs tremble, but the man in the car.

In the relatively small number of years that she had

dated, Tisha had been kissed often, sometimes by boys experienced enough to arouse the natural desire of a woman for a man. The difficult thing to comprehend was the feeling she had that she had only felt the surface fire before and not the white hot heat of desire. What was worse, it had been Roarke's kiss that had generated that discovery. And Tisha had always thought herself immune to physical lust, too ruled by her mind to be betrayed by her senses.

CHAPTER FIVE

TISHA shifted her brush to her other hand and flexed the tense fingers that had been gripping it. Her shoulders sagged as she studied the half-finished painting. It didn't seem to matter what she did today, nothing turned out right.

'Problems?' Blanche asked, the heavy sigh from Tisha drawing her attention.

'Yes, a lack of talent,' Tisha declared disgustedly.

Blanche laid her own brush down and, wiping her hands on a rag, walked over to her niece's side of the studio. Reaching into the pocket of her smock, she took out a cigarette and lit it before placing a hand on Tisha's shoulder.

'What's wrong?' she asked.

Tisha glanced upwards. 'This bouquet is all wrong. It looks as if I'd stuck the violets on a straight line. I did the same thing with the daffodils earlier.' Her shoulders moved in a deprecating shrug. 'I can't do anything right today. I know what I'm doing wrong, but I can't correct it.'

'You can't just learn what your mistakes are, Tish, or you end up only learning mistakes and making them. Discover the right things you do so you can do them more often.'

'Blanche, you are a gem!' The scowl left Tisha's face

as her mouth turned up at the corners in a rueful smile. 'How do you come up with all those pearls of wisdom?'

'Common sense and experience,' smiled Blanche, flicking back the natural white streak in her hair that had fallen forward over her dark brow. 'Experience also tells me that you're as strung up as a high-tension wire. Sometimes tension can stimulate creativity, but in your case it's only causing frustration.'

'What's your suggestion?' asked Tisha.

'Let's take the rest of the afternoon off.' Her brown eyes glanced at the skylight and the windows, continuing from ceiling to floor. 'The light has gone anyway.'

Tisha's own gaze shifted to the windows. Through the panes, she saw the rolling dove-grey clouds that blotted out the early afternoon sun. The tops of the pines were gently swaying, yet there was nothing threatening about the clouds. But the good light was gone, as Blanche had said. Her aunt had returned to her easel and was busy cleaning up her brushes.

A sigh broke from her lips as Tisha followed suit. All her efforts had been wasted motions. Nothing she had done was of sufficient quality for resale. All because of the face that kept dancing in front of her eyes, the face with golden-brown hair and velvet-dark eyes. It would have been so much better if she hadn't gone out with him the night before. She would rather have considered herself a coward for refusing his challenge than face the discovery that he had the ability to sensually arouse her.

'Tisha. Tisha, are you listening to me?'

With a start, she realized Blanche had been speaking to her. 'I'm sorry, I was daydreaming. What did you say?'

'I asked if you'd ever been to the Crater of Diamonds,' her aunt repeated, a curious frown marking her forehead.

'No. A bunch of us were going to go once as a lark, but we never did. Why?'

'I thought we might drive over there this afternoon.'

'To hunt for diamonds?' Tisha laughed shortly, not quite able to visualize her creative aunt digging in the dirt.

'We could,' Blanche agreed with a knowing smile. 'But I had in mind to do some character sketches. A busman's holiday.'

'I'll endorse any suggestion,' adding to herself, 'that will detract my thoughts from Roarke Madison.'

'Everyone has a bad day now and then. Don't let it get you down,' her aunt said. The soothing tone was prompted by the desperate ring in Tisha's voice.

And Tisha could hardly correct her. Blanche liked Roarke and wouldn't understand the abhorrence Tisha felt about the way she kept dwelling on him. Nor could she express her gratitude for the way her aunt had abstained from questioning her about the events of last night, because Tisha wasn't prepared to talk about it.

'I would not change into anything too nice,' Blanche called after her as Tisha started from the studio after straightening her things. 'You might decide to do a bit of grubbing in the earth.'

Tisha thought it unlikely, but she put on a pair of faded jeans and a scooped-neck knit shirt of olive-green. A pale yellow scarf secured her long hair at the nape of her neck and grabbing an equally faded denim jacket from her closet, she wandered outdoors to wait for her aunt.

It was mid-afternoon before Blanche turned her car down the gravelled road carved out of a thick stand of pines. A light breeze whispered through the needles while an Indian summer sun peeped through a cloud and streamed down to lay golden bars on the ground. The stillness surrounding them was so profound that Tisha could almost imagine she and Blanche were the only humans for miles. The rows of cars in the car-park came as something of a surprise.

After paying the nominal entrance fee into the State Park, they followed the path into the cleared, ploughed area. Unlike the other visitors who carried hand tools of claw rakes, small scoops and pans, Tisha and Blanche were armed with sketch pads and pencils. Scattered over the field on each side of the hill were people, singly or whole families, painstakingly sifting through the dark brown soil for diamonds.

Millions of years ago there had been volcanic eruptions near an area covered by water. The sudden cooling of the molten rock by water caused a tremendous pressure that transformed carbon particles into precious diamonds and crystals.

The volcanic pipe, this womb of the only diamonds found in their natural state on the North American continent, was beneath Tisha's feet. It was an exhilarating sensation. The first discovery of diamonds in the 1900s started a rush that threatened to equal the California gold rush. But Tisha also remembered the intrigue that cloaked its past. Attempts to commercially mine the diamonds had been met with frustration, mysterious fires, and even murder before the State of Arkansas finally purchased the Crater of Diamonds outside of Murfreesboro and turned it into a State Park.

Blanche was already seated on the ground with the trunk of a tree for a backrest and her sketch pad propped on her knees. But Tisha was too caught up in the atmosphere of the place to settle down. Instead she wandered down a furrow in the field to where an elderly, grey-haired man was standing hip-deep in a pit he had dug. He was going through the soil, particle by particle, before discarding it on the growing mound beside him.

'Are you having any luck?' Tisha called to him.

He glanced up, blue eyes sparkling above round smiling cheeks. 'Nope!' he answered, tossing the panful of earth away and reaching into his pocket for a handkerchief to wipe his brow. ' 'Course, it would help if I knew what the heck I was looking for!'

'That would be my problem, too,' Tisha laughed.

'They say if you find one you can't mistake it for anything else but a diamond.' He leaned back to rest a

84

moment, obviously welcoming the break and the offer of conversation. 'The problem is to remember that they don't just come in white. There's some that are tinted yellow, brown, pink, and tan. Not to mention they have black diamonds here, too. But when it's a case of finder's keeper's, you can't resist looking. A person might find one.'

'I suppose it's a question of whether Dame Fortune is sitting on your shoulder or not?' she smiled.

'When you realize that nearly all the people out here are amateurs, with maybe a little experience as rockhounds, luck plays an important part,' he nodded agreement. 'But somebody is always finding one.'

'I hope today you're that somebody.'

'The fun is in the looking,' he shrugged, and picked up his shovel.

Tisha wished him good luck and walked further along the furrow, smiling as she found herself studying the ground in anticipation that a diamond crystal might be lying on the top. The diamond fever was contagious, she decided. Just as compelling was the memory of the man's face, roundly smiling and containing such a love of life. While it was still fresh, she found a comfortable rock to lean against and opened her sketch book.

In her first attempt, she couldn't quite capture him and flipped to a fresh page. This time there was no hesitation in the strokes of her pencil as it flew across the paper. Adrenalin seemed to be pumping through her, accenting the exhilarating feeling that she was doing the best portrait she had ever done.

'That's excellent, Tisha!' Blanche exclaimed. While Tisha had been engrossed in her drawing, her aunt had walked silently to stand beside her. 'You've captured Roarke exactly.'

The tip of Tisha's pencil stopped in mid-stroke. The face staring back at her from the paper was Roarke Madison. His mouth was almost curved into a smile. There was that lazy, arrogant look in his eyes. The muscles in her stomach constricted into a sickening knot as Tisha realized what she had done.

Blanche paid no attention to her niece's silence as she began enumerating the successful qualities of the drawing. That hint of a smile is such a great indication of his superb sense of humour. And you've caught the strength and determination in the jawline. I'm amazed, though, at the way you captured the self-assurance that's so much a part of his character.'

'He's arrogant!' Tisha slammed the book shut and scrambled to her feet.

Blanche's brown eyes twinkled with amusement. 'He does make your blood run hot, doesn't he?'

'No!' The denial was out before she realized her aunt was referring to her temper and not desire. Red flames swept into her cheeks. 'I mean yes, we rub each other the wrong way.'

'The chemistry between two people can be compatible or combustible,' her aunt shrugged goodnaturedly. 'With you and Roarke, it's obviously the latter.'

A heavy sigh shuddered Tisha's shoulders. 'Combustible.' That was an excellent word, she thought. She brushed back the tendrils of hair near her forehead and nodded agreement to her aunt's words.

'Don't be so glum,' Blanche teased gently. 'You can't help it if you don't like him.'

Darkly green troubled eyes turned their roundness on the older woman's face. For a moment Tisha hesitated, then the overwhelming need to confide in someone took command.

'Roarke Madison is all the things I don't like in a man – arrogant, argumentative, domineering. Yet,' Tisha swallowed nervously, 'yet he makes me feel more like a woman than any other person I've dated.'

There was a pregnant silence as Blanche studied the embarrassed flush on her niece's face. 'Are you saying that you find him sexually attractive?'

'It doesn't make any sense, I know.' Tisha shifted uncomfortably, her fingers tightening viciously on the sketch pad. 'I don't like him or respect him. Women are a means of entertainment to him. His type doesn't think of them as human beings, only toys to be thrown aside when they no longer amuse him.'

'That's rather a harsh judgment,' Blanche murmured in an effort to placate the vehemence in the younger girl's tone.

'Is it?' Tisha retorted bitterly. 'He's one of those predatory males who charm you into letting your guard down, then rush in for the kill.'

'You've hardly had any time to get to know him.

Aren't you afraid you're being too hasty in condemning him?' At the denial forming on Tisha's mouth, Blanche went on hurriedly but calmly, 'I'm not saying that you're wrong in your opinion of him. Your first meeting with him was under inauspicious circumstances and it's affected your attitude towards him.'

'I think he would have made me bristle no matter how I met him,' Tisha declared.

'That could be true.' A speculative gaze rested on Tisha. 'But it bothers you more to know he arouses you physically, doesn't it?'

The line of her mouth was straight and slightly grim as Tisha nodded an affirmative reply. It made her feel she was betraying herself.

'I wish I knew what to tell you,' Blanche sighed, putting a comforting arm around her niece's shoulders. 'It's something you have to work out for yourself, I guess. What do you say we start for home now? We can stop along the way to eat and save us from fixing a meal tonight. I know a great little restaurant that serves delicious catfish and hush-puppies.'

'That sounds fine,' Tisha agreed, trying to match her aunt's cheerful voice as they jointly turned to retrace their path to the parking lot.

'It looks as if we're going to get some rain from those clouds after all.' The woman's head raised to scan the overcast sky, now a menacing shade of turbulent grey. 'I don't know which I dislike more, driving after dark or driving in the rain.'

'We don't have to stop to eat. It wouldn't be too

much trouble to cook something at home,' Tisha suggested.

'We need the night out,' Blanche insisted. 'Besides, I think the rain will hold off until later this evening and we have ample time before the sun goes down.'

On the drive back, it seemed as though her forecast was going to be correct, but when they walked out of the restaurant, it was into a driving downpour of rain. Blanche willingly accepted Tisha's offer to drive the few miles to the house.

Although the sun wasn't officially down, the black clouds made it appear as dark as night. The rapid lashing back and forth of the windshield wipers couldn't keep up with the onslaught of water. Tisha was glad when they reached the lane leading to home.

'Do you think we dare stop at the mailbox to pick up our mail?' Blanche asked.

'I don't see why not,' Tisha answered. 'The road is firm, so there's no worry that we'll get stuck. I can pull over close enough so all you have to do is roll down the window to reach the box.'

'I was expecting some important letters,' her aunt murmured.

'It's no problem. We'll stop,' Tisha assured her as the car headlights picked out the mailboxes by the side of the road and Tisha slowed the car to a stop beside the first one.

The wind drove the rain inside the car as Blanche hurriedly rolled the window down and stretched her arm out to retrieve the mail, then quickly rolled the window up before she was completely drenched.

'Whew!' she laughed shortly as she shook the water off her exposed arm. 'Let's get home where it's warm and dry.'

Thunder rumbled ominously overhead as Tisha manoeuvred the car into the garage, thankful they had left the doors open, even if it was an invitation to burglars.

'I'm going to have to change out of this blouse,' Blanche said after they had entered the house through the connecting garage door. 'Why don't you put on some coffee?' She lifted the damp garment away from her skin and laughed. 'It's unbelievable I could get so soaked when I only had the window down for a few seconds.'

Tisha was already filling the coffee pot with water. Her shoulders were stiff from the strain of peering through the driving sheets of water.

'Hurry up and change,' she instructed her aunt. 'Or I'll drink this whole pot myself!'

A quarter of an hour later Tisha was snuggled up in the armchair in the living-room, a fresh cup of coffee beside her as she listened to the rain hammering at the window while lightning walked about outside. Blanche had changed clothes and was sitting on the couch going through the mail.

'Oh dear!' Blanche murmured suddenly.

Tisha glanced over and saw her staring at a fairly large package 'Is something wrong?'

'That stupid mailman put this package in the wrong

box,' Blanche sighed impatiently. 'It's Roarke's, and he put it in my box instead of his.'

'You can give it to him the next time you see him, can't you?'

Her aunt nibbled anxiously at her bottom lip. 'I can, yes,' she admitted. 'Except the other night when he came to pick you up. I was talking to him and he mentioned that he had some plans he was supposed to have done by Monday, but he couldn't finish them because he was waiting for some information on a new product. He was hoping it would be in today's mail. And now the mailman's given it to me.'

'That's not your fault.' Tisha couldn't muster any sympathy for Roarke's problem.

'No, but I know he needs it before he can finish. Would you mind running it up to— No, never mind,' Blanche shook her head firmly without finishing the question. 'I'll take it up to him.'

'That's silly. You don't have to run that up to him in this storm!'

'I know he needs it. And I know what it's like to try to finish something and not have the necessary tools or materials,' her aunt insisted, rising to her feet.

'You're really going to take it up to him tonight, aren't you?' Tisha shook her head incredulously. 'As much as you fear driving in this kind of weather, you're going anyway.'

'I know how you feel about him, Tish,' her aunt said as she reached into the closet for her raincoat and umbrella, 'but he is my neighbour and a friend. He would do the same for me, regardless of what you think about him.'

There was a resigned droop to the corners of Tisha's mouth as she realized she wasn't going to be able to persuade her aunt to change her mind. And her conscience wouldn't allow her to let Blanche drive in this kind of weather. As independent and self-sufficient as her aunt was, there were a few things that unnerved her. Two of them were driving in a thunderstorm and after dark.

'If I can't talk you out of it,' she said grimly, reluctantly getting to her feet, 'then I'll take it for you, Blanche.'

'That isn't necessary.'

'I think it is,' Tisha asserted. 'Now put your coat back in the closet and give me the umbrella.'

'I'll ride along with you.'

'There's no need for both of us to go out in this storm.' She bypassed the denim jacket that matched her jeans in favour of her water-repellent windbreaker hanging beside it in the closet. 'You stay home and save me a cup of coffee.'

'Are you sure you don't mind?' Blanche asked anxiously.

'I don't mind,' Tisha breathed in exasperation, and slipped the jacket over her shoulders. 'Where's the package?'

'Here.' Blanche pushed it into her hands. 'And, Tish?'

'Yes?' Tish paused before walking through the

kitchen to the connecting garage door.

'Roarke's house is something of a showplace. It would be worth putting up with his company for a few minutes just to see it.' Blanche didn't allow time for Tisha to reply as she added, 'Drive carefully.'

Tisha thought to herself that the house would have to be pretty fantastic for her to stay. In her present frame of mind, she didn't want to be alone with Roarke. Her attitude towards him was much too ambivalent. Until she was able to control or understand her feelings, the less she saw of him the better it would be.

The heavy downpour forced her to keep the car at a crawling pace as she negotiated the quarter of a mile to Roarke's house. She nearly missed the shrub-bordered driveway entry, her headlights picking it out at the last minute. The rain was creating miniature rivers in the gravelled road while the towering pines seemed like high walls closing in on the car.

Tisha hadn't realized the house was set so far back from the road. Tension closed her grip on the wheel and she knew her knuckles were white. At last a light pierced the gloom, a beacon in the midst of a storm. She parked the car in the small cul-de-sac and switched off the motor. It took some tricky manoeuvring to open the umbrella as she climbed out of the car and dashed through the puddles and driving rain to the overhang. The package was tucked under her jacket in an attempt to protect it from the downpour.

Impatiently she pushed the button to the doorbell. With the growling thunder it was impossible to hear if it was ringing inside. The wind was beginning to beat the rain in about her legs, so Tisha grasped the large brass knocker and began hammering it against the door. In seconds it was opened with Roarke framed in the doorway, wearing a cream pullover sweater and brown slacks.

'Tisha?' His surprise was obvious as he peered under the umbrella. 'I thought only ducks were out in this kind of weather.'

'Quack, quack,' she said sarcastically, fumbling under her jacket for the package.

'You're never at a loss for an answer, are you?' Roarke chuckled. His hand reached out to close over her shoulder and draw her into the shelter of the house. 'I confess that you caught me by surprise. I didn't think you'd miss my company so much that you'd come out on a night like this.'

He had autocratically taken the umbrella from her, half-closing it, and set it against the wall, a puddle of water forming almost immediately beneath it.

'I didn't come to see you,' Tisha retorted angrily. The package was free of her jacket folds and she held it out to him. 'This was put in Blanche's mailbox by mistake. She thought you would need it, so I ran it up here for her.'

The door behind her was already closed. She would have preferred to hand him the package and run. After taking the package, glancing at it briefly, he tossed it on a walnut table.

'Thanks for bringing it, I'd been waiting for it.

Blanche probably remembered,' he smiled. 'Let me take your jacket.'

'I'm not staying.' She backed away as he stepped forward to help her remove it. 'I only came to give you the package. I'll leave now.'

'You can come in by the fire and dry your clothes. I don't think your aunt will miss you if you stay for a few minutes.'

'No, thank you,' she repeated coldly. 'I'll just get wet again when I go back out to the car.'

'I have a whole pot of cocoa made. Are you sure you wouldn't like a cup?' he offered.

'No, I wouldn't.'

'I insist.' Once again his hand closed over her arm before she could elude him. 'It wouldn't be neighbourly to refuse my offer of hospitality in return for you driving through that storm to deliver the package.'

'I really . . .' The protest died away as Tisha sensed that she wasn't going to win the argument. 'Very well, I'll have one cup. Then I'm going to leave.'

'One cup,' he agreed with a patronizing nod of his sandy brown head. He pointed to her right. 'The living-room is in there. I have a fire going in the fireplace. You can dry out a bit while you drink your hot chocolate. By the way, do you like it with marshmallows or whipped cream?'

'Whipped cream, please,' she requested, moving away from him the instant he released her arm.

'Go on ahead. I'll bring the cocoa in a minute.'

Hesitantly Tisha followed his instructions, slowly

walking through the opening he had indicated. Without his presence to distract her, she took in her surroundings, glancing back at the marbled foyer with its white tile floor and light walnut-panelled walls. Then her feet touched the thick, soft pile of a carpet and she looked ahead.

A carved wooden banister beckoned her down a small flight of three steps to a sunken living-room carpeted in a vibrant shade of dark blue. Floor-to-ceiling curtains of knobby white covered almost one entire wall while the rest of the walls alternated between panelling of walnut framing areas of cream-white.

Golden flames leaped behind a dark wrought iron screen in front of the glittering white stone fireplace in the centre of an inside wall. Tisha moved to the middle of the room, fascinated in spite of herself by the artistic perfection of its interior. A large sofa covered in white velour faced the fireplace. The whiteness of its cushions was accented by large pillows in the same bold shade of blue as the carpet beneath her feet. On either side of the fireplace, facing the sofa, were two large chairs with flanking tables, gleaming brightly with the reflected light from the fire.

Blanche had told her Roarke's house was a showplace, but Tisha had truly expected something ostentatious and elegant. Certainly nothing as cosy and inviting as this room was. The luxury was implied, not brazenly displayed.

'Take your jacket off and sit down.'

She turned with a start to see Roarke standing at the

top of the steps.

'If you want more light, there's a dial on the wall by the fireplace,' he motioned with his head since he held a cup in each hand.

That was when she noticed the indirect lighting in the ceiling above. Now its dimness suggested an intimacy that Tisha felt the need to dispel, so she walked with an assumed nonchalance to the dial and turned the light brighter.

'The room is very lovely,' she commented in a tight voice.

'Thank you,' he replied, accepting her compliment with a brief inclination of his head, but Tisha couldn't find any arrogance in the gesture. 'You can turn the chair towards the fire if you like.'

'It's all right,' she assured him nervously as she slipped her arms out of her windbreaker and sat down on the edge of one of the blue-striped chairs. She started to lay the jacket across her lap.

'Let me hang that up for you,' Roarke offered, setting her cup of cocoa on the table beside her.

Reluctantly Tisha gave it up. It was damp and although it wasn't dripping water, she knew the logical thing to do was to put it somewhere where it could dry without getting something else wet in the process. She watched Roarke as he carried her jacket up the few steps before disappearing in the foyer. In seconds he was back. His presence seemed to complete the room, adding the vitality it lacked on its own. As he reclined his lean body on the couch, Tisha picked up her cup, concentrating on the swirling cream floating on top rather than meet his gaze.

The silence began to grow. She swallowed nervously, the crackling of the fire adding to the tension in the air. Somehow she had to speak – about anything.

'Blanche told me your home was beautiful, but I never expected anything like this.'

'What did you have in mind?' Roarke asked dryly.

Tisha glanced over at him, trying to read the veiled expression in his brown eyes. He seemed quite relaxed, yet there was tenseness there, too.

'I suppose I thought it would be . . . more showy,' she replied, trying to adopt an indifferent attitude.

'Gaudy?' An eyebrow quirked.

'I really don't know. I didn't think about it that much,' Tisha shrugged, feeling a surge of retaliatory anger that he should try to put her on the defensive. 'Probably if I had, I would have expected a sofa that made into a bed at the flick of a button while the lights dimmed and soft music filled the room.'

'A perfect setting for a seduction scene, is that it?'

'Something like that,' she agreed, 'but this,' sweeping the air around her with an expressive movement of her hand, 'is much more subtle, although I'm sure it accomplishes the same purpose.'

'Isn't it strange?' Roarke murmured. 'I always looked on this as my home.'

The blandly stated comment curled Tisha's fingers as she carried the cup to her mouth. She heard the reprimand in his words and knew she deserved it for her insult. The hot liquid burned her throat as she tried to drain the cup dry so she could leave. She started when Roarke got to his feet in a lithe movement.

'Come,' he ordered. 'I want to show you the rest of my home.'

'Another time,' she refused quickly, setting her cup down and rising to her feet.

'No,' Roarke said firmly, his tall form blocking her way to the steps, and Tisha had no doubt he would forcibly stop her from leaving. 'I want your impression to be complete.'

She took a deep angry breath. 'Very well.'

'After you.' His outstretched hand signalled her to precede him down the dimly lit hall branching off from the living-room.

Tisha complied, her shoulders squared and stiffly resentful, as she led the way. A few feet into the corridor were two doors directly opposite each other. Roarke opened the one on the right first, turning on the light switch to reveal a blue and green bathroom. Then he moved to the opposite side of the hall and opened the other door.

'This was meant to be the spare bedroom,' he explained, turning on the light and waiting for Tisha to enter the room. 'But I use it as an office and drafting room.'

Just inside the door was a small alcove with closets on each side followed by a set of three steps leading up into the panelled room. Shelves covered one wall with a desk and leather chair in front of them. A drafting table and stool occupied one corner while the rest of the furniture consisted of a leather sofa in a rusty orange colour and a matching recliner chair. The same rusty orange shade was included in the curtains, which also incorporated the blue of the carpet in a bold plaid that completed the masculine, businesslike atmosphere.

Roarke didn't wait for a comment from Tisha as he led her out of the room to the door at the end of the hall. This time he offered no explanation as he opened the door and flicked on the light switch. As Tisha stepped in she realized why. This was the master bedroom – Roarke's bedroom.

There was the same thick blue carpeting on the floor, but here the steps led down where the room was dominated by a large bed covered in a spread of shimmering antique gold. Tisha found it difficult to swallow as her gaze remained riveted to the inviting expanse of the bed to the exclusion of the matching pieces of walnut furniture. She was painfully conscious of Roarke standing beside her.

'It's very nice,' she said abruptly, turning on her heel to escape.

Her pace didn't slow up until she was in the relative safety of the living-room. She glanced back at Roarke, seeing the mockery in his eyes and hating him for it.

'I'd better be going now,' she declared.

'You haven't seen the kitchen yet,' he reminded her with a repressed smile. 'All women are interested in kitchens, aren't they?'

'Show me the kitchen, then,' Tisha snapped.

The marble white tile of the foyer led into the modern kitchen, spacious and efficient. The blue theme of the rest of the house was present in the small yellow and blue flower bouquets of the vinyl paper in a background of cream white. In spite of herself, Tisha was drawn to the homely essence of the room that managed to creep through, but she refused to let it win her.

'As I said before, you have a lovely home.' The insincerity in her voice was a cool wind meant to show her indifference.

'I'm so glad you like it,' Roarke returned with the same hollow enthusiasm. He moved back in the entrance hall where he retrieved her coat from the closet. 'Please thank Blanche for me, won't you? I did have need of the package this week-end.'

'I will,' Tisha nodded, slipping on her jacket and reaching for the umbrella sitting in the corner. She tilted her head back to meet the measured coolness of his eyes. 'And thank you for showing me around.'

He reached around her and opened the door as if he was in a hurry to be rid of her. 'My pleasure,' he taunted.

A stab of lightning illuminated the night as Tisha hurried out the door, more anxious to leave than he was to have her go.

CHAPTER SIX

THE puddles were deeper and the rain was still pouring down. If anything, the storm had increased in intensity as Tisha waded through the running water to her car. When she opened the door and ducked inside, she noticed the headlights of her car illuminating the downpour. Groaning aloud, she tossed the umbrella on the floor beside her and turned the key in the ignition switch. Nothing. Only the click of the key and no answering response from the motor.

Her hands clutched the wheel of the car and she rested her head against them. The battery was dead. She had left the lights on and run down the battery. That meant she had to go back and ask Roarke for help. And that thought didn't appeal to her at all.

With the protection of the umbrella over her head, Tisha sloshed back to the house and banged the knocker against the oak door. This time she didn't have to wait as long for Roarke to answer the door.

'I left the lights on and my battery is dead,' she announced as the door swung open. 'Would you help me get it started?'

He stared at her for a brief moment. 'I'll get my car out of the garage.' Tisha nodded and started to turn away. 'Wait,' Roarke called her back. 'There's no sense getting ourselves drenched trying to start your car tonight. I'll give you a ride home and bring your car back in the morning.'

Tisha started to argue, then changed her mind and again nodded agreement. 'My shoes are wet. I'll meet you by the garage door,' she said, avoiding the suggestion she could see forming on his lips.

She arrived at the double doors just as Roarke began raising them from inside. In seconds she was out of the rain, folding up her umbrella and climbing in the passenger side of the white car. She huddled in her corner while he reversed the car out of the garage and turned it down the lane. Lightning jagged across the sky followed immediately by rolling thunder.

'Well?' Tisha muttered, glancing at the coat sleeve of tan leather. 'Aren't you going to make any comments about women drivers?'

'Why should I?' His head turned briefly towards her. 'You didn't leave your lights on deliberately. It was an honest mistake.'

'But a stupid one,' she grumbled, hating him for the magnanimous way he had dismissed it.

'We all make them. That's what makes us human.' The words were barely out when they were followed by a muffled 'Damn!'

Tisha pushed herself more erectly in her seat, prepared to do battle at the imprecation she thought he had directed at her. Then she felt the application of brakes and glanced ahead. Through the downpour, she could see the reason for his vehement exclamation. A large pine tree had fallen across the road, taking two smaller trees with it.

'Can you move them?' she whispered as she stared at the formidable barrier in the road.

'You can't be serious! Do I look like Superman?' he asked with an accompanying sound that resembled laughter.

'Maybe we can push them out of the way,' Tisha suggested desperately, and fumbled for the handle of the door.

'Forget it,' Roarke barked. He slipped the gear shift into reverse and backed to a wider section of the road and turned the car around.

'Where are you going?' she asked.

'Back to the house,' he answered, his sharp, clipped tones stinging her with their coldness. 'You'll have to stay the night.'

'I'll do no such thing!'

'The road is blocked. We don't have any choice.'

'Oh, yes, we do,' Tisha declared as the lights of the house came into view.

'What brilliant suggestion do you have this time?' He turned the car into the garage and switched off the motor as he brought his gaze around to her.

Her hand closed over the door handle and opened the door. 'I'll walk home!' she declared, scurrying out of the car before the arm that was reaching out for her could stop her.

She fumbled with the umbrella catch while her feet carried her swiftly out of the garage and into the storm. The answering slam of his car door only hurried her movements while the rain began drenching her hair and face.

'Tisha!' Footsteps sloshed through the rain after her. 'Tisha, come back here!'

'I'm going home!' she cried.

Then the umbrella was wrenched from her hands as Roarke pulled her around. The sloppy ground gave her no leverage to struggle with as she uselessly tried to twist free.

'I am not going to let you walk home!' He gave her a vicious shake. 'Now be sensible!'

'No!' She renewed her struggles. 'I'm not going to stay in that house with you!'

'Damn it, Tisha!' Water was pouring down both their faces, making spikes of their lashes and streaming down their necks. 'I didn't put that tree in the road! You're acting as if I'd engineered the whole thing.'

'It isn't so very far to Blanche's. I've walked farther,' she insisted vigorously.

'What happens if a tree falls on top of you, or lightning strikes you?' he demanded.

'Anything would be better than ... than ... I hate you!'

If her own temper hadn't been driving her, Tisha would have seen the building anger in Roarke's face. She would have noticed the tightening of the muscles in his jaw instead of the artificial darkness of his hair glistening wetly in the rain.

With a brutal yank he pulled her against the slickness of his leather jacket. Her arms were pinned against his chest by the force of his hands at her back while her heartbeat tried to keep tempo with the hammering rain.

'You crazy little fool!' he muttered savagely. 'Am I really more dangerous than the storm to you?'

'Roarke, let me go.' It was a weak plea, almost lost in the crash of lightning, and Tisha couldn't tell the difference between the rolling thunder and the pounding of her heart.

'Not Mr. Madison?' His lip curled in sarcasm as his gaze flamed over her upturned face, frightened and pleading with him for mercy.

The denim material of her jeans was plastered against her legs, sapping them of strength with cold dampness, but the crush of his body against her was sending out heat-waves. Yet the violent assault of the elements couldn't match the destruction his embrace was having on her senses. In the midst of the storm, they were isolated from it.

Her lips moved to breathe his name again as she stared into the darkly burning eyes. A hand touched her cheek, pushing back the dark streaks of wet hair that had escaped her scarf before the fingers curled around the back of her neck and Roarke drew her head upward to meet the mouth descending towards hers.

Hungrily Tisha accepted his fierce possession. The bruising pain was no match for the flaming ecstasy that consumed her. There was nothing tantalizing about his kiss this time. He took her mouth with a complete sensuous mastery that turned her bones to water. A desire to be closer to the straining muscles of his body sent her fingers around the buttons of his jacket, releasing them so she could feel for herself the throbbing of his heart. The rain seemed to increase the musky scent of his manhood as Tisha twined her arms around him to force herself closer.

With an agonizing moan Roarke wrenched his mouth away from hers and buried it in her neck, running a trailing fire along the pulsating vein in her throat. She trembled violently, understanding the driving need he felt for her because it was burning inside her, too.

'Roarke,' she murmured achingly, turning her head to seek the hollow of his throat above the cream shade of his sweater.

But the movement of ultimate submission was rejected with a savagery that left her stunned as he thrust her away from him. Rain glistened on the parted sweetness of her lips still swollen from the raging passion of his kiss. She couldn't believe the coldness in his eyes as he glared across the distance that now separated them. A knife of cold steel plunged itself in her heart as she realized he had felt none of the blazing desire she had known. For him the kiss had been a means of punishment for her insults. Only she had read more into it. Racking sobs tore at her chest as she spun around to flee.

'You aren't leaving!' His hand brought her up short again.

'After ... after that, you expect me to stay!' Her voice pierced the night like the cry of a cornered animal.

'I don't expect anything. You're staying!' Roarke clipped out savagely.

'I'd rather be dead than be with you!' Tisha flung at him, tearing at the fingers that gripped her wrist with her free hand.

'You made that point clear before, and it's as meaningless now as it was then.' He retained his grip with ease. 'You're soaking wet. Let's get in the house before you catch pneumonia.'

'No!'

This time she fought him like a wildcat, kicking at him, flailing her arm about his head until he caught it in a vicelike hold. While aiming blows at his legs, she tried to sink her teeth into his hand. Finally he released her wrists and picked her up by the waist, carrying her under his arm like a sack of potatoes to the house. The insults she strung together went unheeded, as did her struggles. Roarke didn't put her down until they were in the foyer and the door was shut behind them.

Her eyes were smouldering dark fires of green as she faced him, her fists rigidly clenched at her side. He was between her and the door and Tisha knew she couldn't get by. Except for the water trickling from his sodden clothes on to the floor, he looked as unruffled as if he had just walked in from the kitchen, whereas she was panting from her exertions to be free.

'You pig!' she spat at him.

'Save your insults for the time when you're capable of defending them,' he returned coldly, slipping off his jacket. 'Give me your coat.'

Tisha stared at him defiantly and Roarke took a threatening step towards her. She hesitated only briefly before angrily ripping the wet windbreaker from her back and throwing it at him. The thin knit top of olive-green was clinging to her like a second skin, accenting the rapid rise and fall of her breasts beneath the scooped neckline.

'Into the kitchen,' he ordered.

Pivoting sharply on her heel, Tisha stalked into the room, knowing Roarke was only one step behind her. She stopped at the table, her fingers closing over the back of a chair as she watched him walk to a cupboard and take out a bottle of drink and two glasses. The door leading to the garage was to her left. She could see it out of the corner of her eye and edged slightly towards it.

His back was still turned to her as he snapped, 'Don't try it!'

'Try what?' Her gaze was defiantly innocent when he turned around.

The line of his mouth mocked her. 'You'd never make it to the garage door and don't tell me that's not what you were planning, because we both know it was.' He poured a shot of amber liquid into each glass, then emptied his in one swallow before picking up the other and walking over to her. 'Drink this.'

Roarke held the glass out to her, but she slapped it away, seeing the liquid slosh out of the glass on to the floor. The muscles in his jaw were working fiercely.

'Somebody ought to take you over their knee,' he muttered.

'Do you always treat your women so brutally?' Tisha jeered.

His eyes narrowed. 'Would you like to find out?'

Pallor robbed her of colour at the undeniable threat in his voice, but she kept her gaze boldly riveted to his, her head tilted back defiantly.

'If you come near me, I'll scratch your eyes out,' she vowed.

'You'd like to do that, wouldn't you?' he chuckled, his dark blond head cocking arrogantly at her puny attempt to threaten him.

'What's the matter? Don't you think I could do it?'

'I think you'd try,' Roarke admitted, walking over to set the mostly empty glass on the counter. 'But don't worry, the only thing I'm interested in is getting out of these wet clothes.'

'Don't let me stop you.'

'I don't intend to.' His gaze lazily moved to her. 'Come on, you're going with me.'

'Where?' Tisha took a hasty step away from him.

'To my bedroom,' he answered grimly. 'That's where I keep my clothes. You need to get out of those wet things, too.'

'Into what? Your bed?' she taunted him.

'That's where all little girls should be at this time of night,' he replied complacently, noting the frightened gleam that appeared in her eyes.

'I'm not going!'

'Do you want me to pick you up and carry you there?'

Tension screamed around her, applying pressure on all sides until Tisha thought she would break in two from the strain. With hate eating away at her mind, her heart was leaping at his potent male virility.

'I want you to stop trying to bully me. I want you to quit ordering me around. I want you to leave me alone!' she cried.

'Stop behaving like an outraged female and accept the fact that you have to spend the night here whether you want to or not!' Roarke retorted.

Tisha was unprepared for the quick movement of his arm as he reached out and pulled her away from the chair she had sought refuge behind. Before she could attempt to struggle free of the hold on her arm he was pushing her away and ahead of him out of the kitchen door, through the foyer, and into the living-room. The hands on her shoulders continued to propel her down the hallway to the door at the end. When she forced him to reach around her to open the door, she tried to bolt past him, but he caught her around the waist and flung her into the room.

Stumbling down the short flight of steps, she turned to face him like a wary animal. She moved hastily backward as he walked down the stairs, but he paid no attention to her poised stance of battle, his supple strides carrying him to the other side of the room.

'The bathroom is through that door behind you,' he drawled, peeling off his sweater and shirt as he opened a set of folding closet doors. 'A good hot shower will drive the dampness out of your bones.'

'What are you going to do?' Tisha ventured in a guarded tone.

'The same thing.' He glanced over his shoulder, an eyebrow elevated in cold mockery. 'Only I'll be in the spare bathroom.'

Sinewy muscles rippled over his broad naked chest as he turned towards her, a pair of dry slacks over one arm. A shiver trembled over her as he came nearer, but again he went past her to a tall chest of drawers.

'There's clean towels hanging inside,' he said. 'I don't have any shower caps, but your hair is already wet, so I don't suppose it makes any difference. And here,' a pair of cranberry silk pyjamas were thrust in her hands as he walked by. 'They'll be too big, but at least they'll be dry.'

'You wear them.' She tried to hand them back to him.

'I don't mean to shock you, Red,' he smiled without amusement, 'but I don't wear pyjamas in bed. Now go and take your shower.'

She coloured furiously. 'I don't want to take a shower. I don't want your clothes. And I don't intend to go to bed!'

Roarke stopped and turned back to her, his jaw set in an uncompromising line. 'Let's get something straight. You're going to take a shower if I have to strip you and shove you in there myself. And unless you want to walk around in a skimpy bath towel, you're going to wear those pyjamas. Lastly, you're going to go to bed. So no more arguments.'

With his ominous decree ringing in the air, he walked over to a smaller chest and took out a pillow and some blankets.

'What are you doing?' she demanded.

'Since I'm going to be sleeping on the couch, I thought I might like some covers,' he answered shortly before a wicked glint appeared in his eyes. 'Or were you going to offer to share the bed with me?'

'You're disgusting!' Tisha declared vehemently.

'Am I?' Roarke taunted.

'You're despicable and arrogant!' she added.

'Is that all? Never mind,' he waved off the words that had started to spring to her mouth. 'Go and take your shower before you catch cold.'

'I hope you get pneumonia and die!' she called after him as his long strides carried him up the steps to the hallway door.

But the door closed with a finality that left Tisha with the impression that Roarke was glad to get her out of his sight. For a moment she stood there, the silence of the room closing in around her, muffling the growls of thunder outside the window. A shuddering chill quivered over her as the dampness of her clothes began to seep into her bones. However reluctantly, she had to admit that the tingling spray of a hot shower would feel good.

With the pyjamas still clutched in her hand, Tisha walked into the gold and blue bathroom, locking the door behind her. For several minutes she stood motionless under the biting spray as it beat out the embittered anger that had strained her nerves to the breaking point. When she finally stepped out of the shower stall and towelled herself dry, she was left with a self-pitying shame that she had responded with desire to the punishing passion of Roarke's kiss.

Going through the motions of hanging up her wet clothes, she fought off the aching void in her stomach, telling herself she was glad he had rejected her advance before she had suffered the ultimate humiliation. If anyone had tried to tell her that she could feel such lust for a man she didn't like, she would have called them a liar, but her own actions had proved her wrong. No matter how hard she tried, she couldn't wholly blame Roarke for the misery that was drowning her with its waves of self-sorrow.

Determinedly she brushed away the teardrops hovering on the tips of her lashes. She wrapped her long hair in a towel and piled it on top of her head as she reached for the pyjama top. The silk material felt cool and slippery against her skin, but sleeves hung far below the tips of her fingers. It took some time to fight the excessive length and roll them up to a point where her hands were free. With the buttons buttoned, the ends of the pyjama shirt stopped a few inches above her knees. One glance at the pants and Tisha knew they were miles too long and too big around the waist, so she simply folded them back up and laid them on the counter.

Unlocking the door, she re-entered the bedroom and

walked to the gold-covered bed. She ignored the invitation of its empty width to sprawl herself across it and cry out the misery she felt for herself. Instead she found a spot near the edge and sat in a cross-legged position with her back to the door. Unwrapping the towel from her head, she began vigorously rubbing her long hair dry.

A knock on the door was followed immediately by Roarke calling out, 'Are you decent?'

'What do you want?'

But the door opened without an answer and Roarke walked in. He still wore only a pair of trousers, but they were wheat tan instead of the brown pair he had had on before. The light colour accented the dark tan of his chest. Tisha watched him from over her shoulder as he walked to the top of the steps.

'I brought you some cocoa to help you relax and get some sleep.' His face wore an inscrutable expression as his dark eyes flicked over Tisha.

'How thoughful!' she mocked coldly, turning away from him to continue rubbing her hair with the towel.

'There'll be a crew out in the morning to clear the road, and I telephoned Blanche to let her know I was putting you up for the night,' he continued without the slightest pause at her sarcasm.

Tisha had been so busy feeling sorry for herself that she had completely forgotten that her aunt might be concerned about her prolonged absence.

'Thank you.' Reluctant gratitude edged her voice.

'Do you want this cocoa or not?'

She could tell that he was still standing on the landing. It would have been quite simple to walk over and take the cup from him, but she didn't care to meet the freezing indifference of his gaze.

'You can put it on the bedside table. I'll drink it later,' she replied, keeping her head averted as she heard his footsteps moving down the stairs towards the bed. Through the shield of her long hair, she saw him walk by her without a glance. When he turned to retrace his steps, she asked, 'Is there a comb I can use to get these tangles out of my hair?'

'There's probably one in the medicine cabinet.'

'Thanks,' she said shortly, uncurling a long leg from beneath her to slip off the bed.

She was half-way to the bathroom when his voice barked out at her. 'Where's the bottoms of those pyjamas?'

She stopped and glanced back at him, surprised at the restrained fury on his face. 'They were too big,' she shrugged.

'Put them on,' Roarke ordered.

'I told you they were too big!' she repeated angrily, bristling at his censorious tone.

'And I told you to put them on. What are you trying to do – look like some silly sex kitten?' he jeered.

Bitter tears burned at her eyes as she glared at the tall figure halted just short of the steps. 'The last thing I would try to do is entice you,' she hurled back at him. 'I told you they were too big for me, but don't take my word for it.'

Spinning around, she stalked into the bathroom and slammed the door, grabbing the bottom half of the pyjamas from the counter. Fighting the long legs, she finally managed to draw the waist around her chest while her feet wiggled through the material folds to touch the furry carpet. She shuffled over to the door and swung it open.

'Do you see what I mean?' she demanded, looking from Roarke to the baggy material of the trousers lying in layers around her feet.'

'Roll up the cuffs,' he growled.

'Fine.' A mocking smile of sweetness curved her mouth. 'What do I do about the waistline? You're not exactly a size ten!'

'Improvise,' he snapped.

'Improvise. You're absolutely impossible! What's wrong with wearing only the top? The darned thing nearly comes to my knees. What's so indecent about that?'

Tisha took two angry strides in his direction. On the third the material tangled about her feet and catapulted her forward. Her arms reached out ahead of her to break the fall, but her hands encountered Roarke's arms and chest as he tried to catch her. Off-balance, they both tumbled to the floor, Roarke's body acting as a cushion as Tisha fell on top of him.

'Are you hurt?' he asked, gently rolling her off him on to the carpeted floor.

'No,' she gasped, momentarily winded by the shock of the fall. 'No thanks to you.'

'Was I supposed to let you dive head first on to the floor?' he muttered.

'You shouldn't have made me put on these stupid pyjama bottoms,' she retorted, suddenly conscious of the heat of his body against hers. 'I told you they were too big, but you wouldn't listen to me.'

'Well, that's spilt milk now,' Roarke declared angrily, reaching over her to place his hand on the floor and lever himself upright.

His arm accidentally brushed her breast. Tisha sharply drew in her breath at the intimate contact. That jellylike weakness spread through her bones as he turned his enigmatic gaze on her. He was propped inches above her, his bared chest with its curling dark hairs intimidating her with his closeness. The desire to touch him came dangerously near the surface and Tisha turned her head sharply away, a solitary tear trickling out of the corner of her eye.

'Tisha—'

'Oh, go away and leave me alone!' Her voice crackled slightly on the last word.

His fingers closed over her chin and forced her head around to where he could see the angry fire blazing in her eyes.

'Haven't you humiliated me enough?' she demanded hoarsely.

'You green-eyed little witch,' Roarke muttered.

His gaze was focused on her parted, trembling lips. A horrified 'No!' escaped her mouth as she brought up her hands to ward him off.

The instant her fingers touched the burning hardness of his naked chest, Tisha knew her body was going to betray her again. When his mouth closed over hers, she succumbed to the rapturous fire that swept through her veins. The hands that had moved to resist him twined themselves around his neck while his hands trailed down to her waist deftly arching her towards him.

Her nerves were attuned to every rippling muscle of his body as they responded to his searching caress. It was a seduction of the senses, mindlessly destroying all cognizance of her surroundings except for his touch. An almost silent sound of shuddering ecstasy came from her throat as he pushed the pyjama top away from her shoulder and started a liquid trail of fire over her skin while his mouth sought out the hollow of her throat.

'You're a witch,' he murmured against her lips, then moved to nibble her ear lobe.

Tisha moved protestingly beneath him, her breath stolen by his ceaseless caresses yet needing the fire of his lips against hers. Her hand began a sensuous exploration of his back and shoulders, their nakedness inflaming her desire. His mouth moved over hers, lingering for precious seconds before he raised his head, his hands closing over her arms and pulling them away.

In one fluid movement, Roarke was on his feet, grasping her hands to pull her to his side, leaving the oversized pyjama bottoms on the floor. Her rounded green eyes raised their lashes to look at him, afraid of the cold rejection of before, but this time finding smouldering fires that threatened to blaze again.

'Do you have any idea what you do to a man?' he asked. His fingers closed over her shoulders, holding her in front of him while keeping her safely away.

Tisha was still trembling from the shock waves he had produced and could only look at him numbly. With one part of her mind, she seemed to sense the effort he was making to control his emotions.

'Drink your cocoa and go to bed.' A finger lightly touched her lips as he walked determinedly towards the door. He stopped midway up the steps and looked back. 'When I leave, put the chair under the doorknob. There isn't any lock.'

'I trust you,' she whispered.

'Thanks,' he answered dryly, 'but at the moment I don't trust myself, so do as I say.'

'Yes, Roarke,' Tisha nodded, surprised by her own meekness.

'Another thing,' his gaze moved possessively over her, 'there's no need to bother wearing the rest of those pyjamas, I already know what you look like without them.'

She smiled timidly, not wanting him to leave but afraid to have him stay. 'Good night.'

'Good night, Tisha.'

'Have a nice night.'

'More than likely I'll go quietly out of my mind.' A lazy smile moved across his face as he opened the door. 'And don't forget about the chair.'

'I won't,' she promised.

But she did. Somehow she knew it wouldn't be necessary.

CHAPTER SEVEN

Tisha rolled over on her stomach, burying her head in the pillow to fight off the wake-up call of her conscious. A deliciously warm sensation of contentment was enveloping her and she didn't want to break its spell. An eyelid flickered open of its own volition and a green eye focused on the cranberry silk material covering her arm.

Vividly her mind recalled the events of the night before when Roarke had aroused the latent core of passion within her, then had left without satisfying it. Was she glad? she wondered, blinking open both eyes as she shifted on to her back. She stared at the sunlight sifting through the curtains. Yes, she decided, she was glad. There was no doubt in her mind that she had disturbed Roarke physically. But was it because she was an attractive woman or because she was Patricia Caldwell?

A little sigh escaped her lips at the unanswerable question. For the moment she didn't want to try to figure out the whys and wherefores. There was time enough for that later. At the moment she wanted only to find Roarke, to see if the bright light of day would change her reactions towards him and vice versa.

A little reluctantly she slipped out from under the covers and padded into the bathroom. Her clothes from the night before were dry and she hurriedly put them on. It took several minutes to untangle the sleep-caused snarls in her hair. There was too much electricity in it for her hair to lie neatly about her shoulders and the scarf was much too wrinkled from last night's drenching. A search of her pockets revealed a pair of fasteners, and Tisha divided her hair into pigtails.

Softly humming a happy tune, she hurried from the bedroom, alertly listening and looking for a sign of Roarke. An overhead light shone from the open doorway of his den, slowing her steps as she neared it. When she glanced into the room, she saw Roarke slouched over the drafting table, his head cradled in his arms and a blanket thrown over his shoulders. The song in her throat died as her feet carried her into the room.

There was a compelling urge to walk over and push back the wayward strand of light brown hair from his forehead. In sleep he looked less formidable and, if possible, more attractive. As her hand closed over the railing to guide her up the steps, Tisha saw him move. The carpet had muffled the sound of her footsteps and she knew he couldn't have heard her enter. Still he wakened, propping his hands up with his elbows while they wearily rubbed his face. Any moment now he would notice her presence in the room.

'Good morning,' Tisha greeted him brightly.

Her legs were no longer able to carry her up the steps as he turned a scowling face towards her.

'Is it?' he mumbled testily as he stiffly moved his protesting shoulders.

'It's not raining,' she added hesitantly.

But he seemed not to hear her. A large hand rubbed his mouth and chin. 'I don't suppose you've made any coffee,' he grumbled.

'I've only just got up,' Tisha defended herself.

'Well, go and make some.'

The fragile bubble of happiness burst. Except for one frowning glance, he hadn't even looked at her.

'I will make coffee because I would like a cup,' she declared icily. 'If you want one, you can come out to the kitchen and get it!'

She spun angrily around and stalked from the room. The slamming of a few cupboard doors later, she had filled the electric percolator with water, found the coffee, plugged it in, and was sitting stiffly in a chair listening to the bubbling sound.

The coffee pot was heaving its last dying sigh when Roarke entered the kitchen. Without looking directly at him, Tisha noticed he had shaved, restored his hair to some semblance of order, and donned a brown silk shirt to go with his pale tan slacks.

'The coffee's done,' she announced, rising to pour herself a cup and carrying it over to the table, but she didn't offer to pour him one.

'Do you want juice, toast, or anything?' he asked.

'No, thank you,' she answered coldly.

'Well, don't bite my head off,' Roarke shot back.

'Don't snap at me, then,' darting him an angry glance. 'If you sat up all night working instead of going to sleep, don't take it out on me!'

123

His gaze pierced the air between them. 'The couch happens to be five and a half feet long. My driver's licence says I'm six feet two. You try sleeping in those circumstances.'

'It's not my fault,' she shrugged airily.

'As I recall, you were sleeping in the only available bed,' he pointed out, leaning negligently against the kitchen counter while he sipped at the steaming coffee in his cup.

'You could have—'

'I could have what?' he asked with deadly quiet.

Tisha rose hastily to her feet, hot colour washing over her cheeks as she moved past him to refill her cup. 'You could have slept in the bed and I could have taken the couch,' she finished.

He set his cup on the counter and reached out to halt Tisha in front of him. That aching void returned to the pit of her stomach as his eyes wandered over her.

'Or I could have slept in the bed with you,' Roarke murmured.

'I didn't say that,' she breathed.

His hands moved to her waist, drawing her closer to him. 'But I could have stayed with you, couldn't I?'

A chill of longing quivered through her at the husky, caressing quality in his voice. Her head bowed in mute affirmation of his statement.

'And if I had,' Roarke went on, 'this morning you would have been trying to find a way to attach strings.'

A cold chill seared her heart. 'Is that why you didn't?' she demanded, tossing her head back with injured pride. 'Because you were afraid I would turn into a clinging female?'

'Don't pretend experience where there is none,' he admonished with a mocking tilt of his head.

'Since you prefer experience,' she said sarcastically, her rigid body trembling with his dismissal of her abilities, 'why did you bother to kiss me? Were you just making sure you hadn't lost the knack?'

'No.' Roarke shook his head gently. 'When a female becomes all soft and yielding beneath his touch, a man's reaction is instinctive. And for all the biting lash of your tongue, Red, you're a desirable woman.'

'At least you don't find me totally objectionable,' she snapped.

'I don't find you objectionable,' he assured her calmly. 'The truth is the exact opposite.'

'You're talking in circles. I don't understand anything you're saying,' she cried. 'One minute you say I'm too naïve for you and in the next you imply that you want me. Can't you make up your mind?'

'Yes, I can.' His voice underlined the personal pronoun. 'But what about you? How do you feel towards me?'

'At the moment I hate you!' she retorted angrily.

His hand moved in a suggestive caress over her hips. 'Yes, last night you would have allowed me to make love to you.'

A sigh of confusion broke from her lips as the anger dissolved away. Her troubled eyes sought his face, a helpless whirl of dismay in her own expression.

'It's crazy, isn't it?' she murmured. 'I hate you and I—' The rest of the sentence became stuck in her throat.

'Careful,' Roarke warned. The teasing glint left his eyes as they darkened with black fires. His hands automatically tightened, drawing her to him until the muscles of his thighs met the contact of her softer, feminine form. 'I might hold you to any admission you make.'

Tisha wasn't sure what that admission would have been. Love couldn't happen this quickly, nor allow her to feel such burning antagonism towards him.

'In one form or another, Roarke,' she spoke softly, 'we're a combustible combination.'

'I couldn't agree with you more.'

The smile on his face amplified the satisfaction in his eyes as his hands moved up her back, pulling her against him while his mouth started another fire against hers. The contact was tenderly possessive and intimate, and ended too soon. But the comforting warmth of his arms held her against him as he nuzzled her hair.

'Good morning, Tisha. I don't believe I've said that yet, have I?' he murmured.

'No.' She smiled against his chest, no longer caring about her ambivalent reactions to him. She tilted her head back to look at him. 'Are you always such a grouchy old bear when you get up in the mornings?'

'Only when I've had a girl running around half-naked in my bedroom the night before,' he grinned.

The look in his eyes turned her legs to rubber.

There was a click of a door latch and Tisha felt Roarke stiffen beside her. With a curious turn of her head, she glanced towards the door connecting the kitchen with the garage. Shock held her motionless for a full second.

'Dad!' she squeaked in disbelief, wrenching herself guiltily from Roarke's arms. She stared into the cold fury of her father's face, but he had eyes only for the man beside her. 'What are you doing here?' she breathed.

His eyes shot her a look of chilling disgust and Tisha knew with cold certainty exactly what he was thinking. Red flames of embarrassment scalded her cheeks.

'Dad, it's not the way you're thinking,' she rushed. 'I had to stay last night because there was a tree blocking the road and ... and I couldn't walk home in that storm.'

'That's funny,' he murmured sarcastically. 'There wasn't any tree in the road when I drove up here.'

The challenge in his eyes was unmistakable as he glared at Roarke, who was still leaning calmly against the counter, his gaze frankly meeting the open hostility of her father's.

'A road crew was supposed to clear it this morning.' Her hand moved nervously around her throat. 'They ... they must have already done it.'

Blanche appeared in the doorway, her sympathetic eyes seeking Tisha out immediately. 'I'm sorry, darling,' she murmured. 'He arrived this morning. I couldn't stop him.' Her hands were upraised in a help-less gesture.

'Your name is Madison, isn't it?' Richard Caldwell demanded, and Roarke inclined his head in an affirma-tive movement. 'Patricia, I want you to drive Blanche back to the house.'

'Father, stop this!' she cried. 'You're acting like some Victorian father. All you need is a shotgun! Nothing happened last night. Roarke, explain to him!'

'Yes,' her father challenged, 'I'm sure that intimate little scene I witnessed when I walked in was only a demonstration of your brotherly affection for my daughter!'

'It wasn't intimate!' Tisha protested, stamping her foot angrily on the floor. 'He was only holding me in his arms.'

'I told you to leave!' The thread holding her father's temper snapped.

'No!' She planted herself firmly in his path. 'Not until you accept our explanation.'

'I don't need your explanation! I knew what had been going on when I walked into the room!'

'For heaven's sake, Dad, I'm your daughter. Won't you listen to me?' Despair and frustration rimmed her voice. Then her mouth turned down in a grim line. 'Or is it because I'm your daughter? Because you know what you would have done in the same circumstances?'

A glimmer of guilt flickered across his face before he quickly blacked it out. 'That's sheer nonsense!' he blus-tered. 'And don't try to sidetrack me.'

'I'm not trying to sidetrack you. I'm trying to keep you from making a fool of yourself and me!'

Richard Caldwell stared at her for a long minute, resisting the plea in her tear-filled, angry green eyes. His hard gaze drifted towards Roarke, who was still quietly watching the proceedings.

'Mr. Madison and I are going to have a private talk,' her father declared in a controlled tone. 'I want you to get in your car and go home with Blanche.'

'I can't. The battery is dead in my car,' Tisha retorted, maintaining her mutinous stand in front of him.

'Then take my car!' he snapped.

She folded her arms and continued to glare at the tall, dark-haired man. 'I'm supposed to be the wronged party in this farce. Surely I'm entitled to listen to this "private conversation"?'

'Females can't discuss things intelligently when their emotions are involved. You'd start getting hysterical,' he stated forcefully.

'Oooh!' The angry sound was ripped from her throat. 'You're the one who can't discuss things intelligently! You weren't even here last night, yet you're so positive you know everything that happened!'

'I will not tolerate your insolence any longer!' her father exploded. 'You will leave this house now!'

'I am not leaving you here alone with Roarke!' Tisha exclaimed, raising her voice to match the level of her father's.

There was a slight sound of movement behind her, then a hand was touching her waist. 'I'm capable of fighting my own battles, Red,' Roarke drawled in an amused tone.

'I was beginning to think you were the type that hid behind a woman's skirt,' Richard Caldwell jeered.

Over her shoulder, Tisha saw the sudden narrowing of Roarke's eyes, although his expression remained outwardly bland. From her own experience, she knew Roarke was a formidable opponent. She had never been able to get the best of him even though there were times when she thought she had.

'I appreciate your concern over last night's events, Mr. Caldwell,' Roarke replied with amazing calm. His glance slid down to Tisha with a reassuring glint in the depths of his brown eyes. 'And I quite agree that it will be difficult to discuss this rationally with your daughter's temper erupting all over the place.'

She gasped at his sudden betrayal of her. 'I am not leaving!'

'Go on.' He gave her a little shove. 'Take Blanche home. I'm certain your father and I can come to some understanding.'

This time she turned her rebellious stand to him, tilting her head back to glare at him defiantly. 'I won't go.'

'You will do as your father wishes,' Roarke stated in a very quiet and very firm tone.

'And if I don't, what will you do – pick me up and carry me out to the car?' Her voice trailed away on the last word as the look in his eyes reminded her of last night when he had unceremoniously carried her into the house.

'If necessary,' he murmured.

Tisha was defeated and she knew it. One glance at her father saw the glimmer of respect in his eyes at the authoritative tone of Roarke's voice. He would probably applaud as Roarke carried her bodily out of the house if she continued to resist.

The venom on her tongue was divided equally between the two men. 'I think both of you are disgusting with your highhanded, arrogantly right male airs! I'm leaving, but it's because I can't stand the sight of either of you!'

Bitter tears burned her eyes as she marched out of the kitchen with her aunt trailing quietly along in her wake. At her father's car, she paused, then walked around to the passenger's side.

'You drive, Blanche,' she commanded tightly. 'I'm so mad I'd probably run us into a tree.'

Her teeth were making marks in her knuckles as her aunt started the car and turned it down the lane. Hot tears of frustration scalded her cheeks.

'I've never been so humiliated in all my life,' she muttered. 'Why did Dad have to show up? Why is he always ready to believe the worst?'

'He missed you, Tisha,' her aunt murmured softly. 'He drove up to spend the day with you.'

'Well, I wish he hadn't come. I never want to see him again!' she declared angrily. Her shoulders sagged in defeat. 'I didn't mean that. He's my father and I love him,' she sighed, brushing the tears from her face.

'But why can't he trust me?'

'It isn't you so much that he doesn't trust. It's Roarke.' A small smile of half-humour flitted across her aunt's mouth. 'Let's face it, if Roarke had been sixty years old and podgy, your father would have never jumped to the conclusions that he did. And if he walked in, as you said, and found you in Roarke's arms, you can't blame him for jumping to the obvious. You have to remember your father is a man who probably swept aside many a woman's objections. He most likely imagined Roarke doing the same thing with you.'

A wave of shame washed over her. Only Tisha, and Roarke, too, knew how close her father's accusations had come to being the truth. Guilt was undoubtedly the reason her denial of her father's implications had been so vehement and perhaps less believable.

'If only that tree hadn't blown down last night,' Tisha sighed, accompanying the sound with a grimace. 'And the road crew hadn't so promptly cleared it away this morning.'

'If only I hadn't sent you up here last night with that package,' Blanche reminded her dryly. 'I was the one who insisted that it had to be taken up last night.'

'Oh, Blanche, I don't blame you,' she asserted quickly.

'I know you don't,' Blanche smiled, parking the car in front of her house. 'I left the coffee on.'

'I hope it's strong and black,' Tisha declared, opening her car door and stepping out, 'because I could sure use it!'

Inside the house, Blanche poured them each a cup of coffee and carried it to the kitchen table where they sat in silent commiseration. A heavy sigh wrung itself from Tisha's lips.

'After what's happened, I don't imagine Dad will let me stay here. He'll probably pack me up and take me home where he can keep me under lock and key. If I thought he intimidated my dates before, it will be nothing compared to what he'll do now,' she said with a resigned shake of her head.

'You don't have to leave,' Blanche assured her firmly. 'No matter what my brother says you're welcome to stay.'

'Thanks,' Tisha smiled, her gaze straying out the window. 'What do you suppose he's going to do to Roarke?'

'I doubt that he'll do anything to him,' her aunt said wryly.

'I wish I knew what was going on up there.'

'We'll soon find out,' Blanche stated.

It was over an hour later before they heard the sound of Tisha's car coming up the drive. She exchanged a sympathetic glance with her aunt as she prepared to meet the fury of her father. When he walked into the kitchen, there was a very satisfied smile on his face. He rubbed his hands together as if he had just successfully completed a very difficult mission.

'Is there any coffee left?' he asked cheerfully.

Tisha had expected anything but this seeming good nature. A puzzled frown creased her forehead as she watched him pour himself a cup of coffee and carry it to the table where she and Blanche were sitting.

'You're a very lucky little lady,' he nodded at her as he straddled a chair at the end of the table. The sun winked over the silver wings of his hair near the temples.

'What do you mean?' Tisha asked warily.

'Your Mr. Madison has agreed to do the right thing by you,' he announced smugly, taking a sip of the scalding liquid.

Her back stiffened at his words. 'What do you mean? The right thing?'

'He's agreed to marry you, of course!'

'Oh, my God!' Stunned disbelief held her paralysed. 'You can't be serious!'

'You're damned right I'm serious,' he declared. 'We'll get the blood tests and the marriage licence this week.'

'No!' Tisha cried. 'No, no, no, no! I'm not going to marry him!' She jumped to her feet in frustration.

'You most certainly are!'

'I don't even know the man,' she protested with a desperate cry. 'As a matter of fact I don't even like him!'

'You should have realized that before you spent the night with him.'

'I spent the night at his house, but not with him. Surely he explained that? He did, didn't he?' Fear gripped her throat as she waited for her father to answer.

'Actually there was no reason to discuss the exact details of what happened last night,' he shrugged complacently. 'As soon as I discovered his intentions towards you were honourable, there wasn't any need to go into his intimate knowledge of you.'

'His intentions were honourable!' Tisha repeated. 'Do you mean Roarke does want to marry me?'

'I persuaded him that he should, and with all possible haste.'

'Richard, did you threaten to bring charges against him?' Blanche demanded angrily.

'Not in so many words,' he shifted uncomfortably. 'But the man is intelligent. He understood I had to protect my daughter's reputation. And of course, he had to protect his against the possibility of scandal.'

'You're actually going to force me to marry him!' Tisha cried. 'I don't love him!'

'He's a very personable young man with an excellent career. Fairly wealthy too, from what I was able to determine. You could do very much worse. Kevin would never have been able to handle you, but I think Madison would be able to keep you in line,' her father asserted. There was a sparkle of fire in his eyes when he looked at her. 'When I walked in that kitchen, you were very willingly in his arms and he had just kissed you, too. You may not be in love with him now, but with a man like that, it will come in time.'

'No,' she breathed helplessly, 'I am not going to marry him!'

'The matter has been settled, and we won't discuss it

any further.' He set his cup on the table and rose from his chair. 'Now, if you'll excuse me, I'm going to have to start making arrangements to be free this week. That's one of the blessings of being your own boss. In cases of emergency, you can delegate the work to your employees.'

'I don't believe it,' Tisha murmured, sinking into her chair as her father walked from the room. 'How could Roarke agree to this?'

'I'm as surprised as you are,' confessed Blanche.

'I keep feeling this is a nightmare and if I could only pinch myself hard enough I would wake up. Thank heaven for all the modern formalities you have to go through before there can be a marriage. Dad would have had us married on the spot!' Tisha shuddered. 'I always knew he was terribly old-fashioned, but I never dreamed he would resort to this.'

'Roarke has obviously agreed to this ... marriage,' her aunt said hesitantly. 'Physically I know you attract him. I was wondering ... have you fallen in love with him?'

'Me? In love with Roarke?' In spite of all the indignation Tisha put in her voice, the negative shake of her head was one of uncertainty. 'Never!' she added firmly, partially afraid to examine her emotions. She rose quickly to her feet again. 'I have to speak to Father. Somehow I have to make him understand that I won't marry Roarke!'

CHAPTER EIGHT

FOR the rest of the morning and the better part of the afternoon, Tisha argued and pleaded with her father. Neither tears nor logic nor anger could persuade him to change his mind. She knew she would not be able to move him from his adamant stand as long as he believed that Roarke would marry her. She stormed into the studio where Blanche had discreetly retreated to allow them privacy.

'Please, go and keep Dad occupied,' Tisha pleaded, bitter tears of frustration scalding her eyes. 'I have to call Roarke, and I don't want Dad accidentally picking up the phone and finding out.'

Blanche immediately set down her brush and began wiping her hands on a rag. 'No luck?' she asked sympathetically, and the grim expression on her niece's face gave her a wordless answer of the futility of her attempts. 'Roarke's number is in the address book by the telephone.'

Tisha sent a clipped thanks to her departing aunt and walked to the telephone. With fingers trembling with anger, she dialled the number and listened impatiently to the rings that went unanswered. She was all ready to slam down the receiver when she heard Roarke's voice.

'Where have you been?' she demanded angrily.

'Who is that? Tisha?'

'Of course,' she snapped.

'Yes, of course.' There was dry amusement in his voice. 'Who else would greet anybody that rudely? As to where I've been, I work for my living, you know.'

'I haven't got time for idle conversation,' Tisha retorted. The husky, mocking sound of his voice added more fuel for her fiery temper to feed on. 'Father might find out any minute that I'm calling you.'

'After what he already suspects, what harm is there in a telephone call?'

'Just shut up and listen! Father is always in bed by ten o'clock. I want you to meet me at eleven sharp down at the end of the lane. Have you got that?'

'Yes—'

She cut in on the rest of his words, 'I'll see you there,' and hung up the telephone. This was not the time for long-drawn-out conversation.

Tisha stayed clear of her father until the evening meal, where she maintained an icy coolness and occasionally tossed barbed remarks at him so he would know she still did not accept his edict of marriage. But nothing shattered his resolve that he was doing the right thing. By the time she and Blanche had cleared the table her father had retreated to the living-room, she was beginning to wonder if there was any way to elude the proposed wedding ceremony short of running away. Roarke was the key to the solution, she decided, immersing her hands in the dishwater. Between the two of them, they would come up with a way out of this mess.

Her gaze wandered idly to the window above the sink. With a start, Tisha recognized the white sports car pulling to a stop in front of the house. A glance at the clock told her it was only a few minutes past seven o'clock. Surely Roarke hadn't misunderstood her. She had said eleven, not seven.

The dish in her hand slid back into the water as she reached for the towel in her aunt's hand. 'It's Roarke! He's here now!' she exclaimed in a panicked whisper.

'I thought you said you were going to meet him at eleven,' Blanche frowned.

'That's what I told him.' Only the excess water was wiped from her hands. 'I have to stop him before Dad sees him!'

Before she was half-way across the kitchen, the door-bell rang. Richard Caldwell was already at the front door by the time Tisha reached the kitchen archway. She stopped in its frame, poised to take flight as she watched the calm, almost friendly way the two men greeted each other. Her heart was lodged somewhere in the vicinity of her throat, pulsing wildly at the sight of the tall composed man exchanging pleasantries with her father.

'I hope you don't mind me dropping in this evening,' he was saying in a condescending voice. His brown eyes glittered momentarily at Tisha. 'I wanted to speak to your daughter. May I see her alone?'

Her father followed his gaze to Tisha, a triumphant gleam lighting their depths. 'I have no objection.'

'Would your sister's studio be all right?' Roarke inquired with correct politeness that grated Tisha's already raw nerves.

'Certainly,' her father agreed.

If Tisha hadn't wanted so badly to see Roarke and put an end to this talk of a marriage between them, she would have refused outright to see him. As it was, she was forced to lead the way to the studio.

The instant the door was closed behind them, she turned on Roarke with a vengeance. 'I told you to meet me at eleven o'clock!' she hissed.

'You didn't think I was going to fall into that trap again?' he drawled coldly.

Unconsciously she stiffened at his slashing tone, staring into the unrelenting hardness of his carved face with a confused frown on hers.

'What trap?'

'This has to be the oldest trick in the book. I expected something more original from you, Red.' One hand was hooked in the waistband of his trousers as his arrogant gaze insolently raked her slender body, ignoring the bewildered expression in her eyes.

'What are you talking about?'

A twisted smile lifted one corner of his mouth. 'I wonder how many men have been trapped into marriage after spending a night with a girl, however innocently, while the outraged father appears on the doorstep in the morning.'

With a gasp of dismay, Tisha realized he thought she had planned the whole thing. 'You don't think that I—' she rushed. 'You can't believe that I engineered this! I swear to you I had no idea my father would be coming to visit me today. I never intended any of this to happen. Roarke, you've got to believe me!' The last desperate flurry of words brought her closer to his imposing figure while her eyes pleaded with him.

'My dear girl,' a sardonic glint appeared in his eyes, 'if I thought for one moment that you'd arranged this, I would wring your neck.'

For a moment, Tisha was unable to believe that his accusation had been in jest. Then the ghost of suppressed laughter glittered in his eyes.

'This is no time to be joking!' stamping her foot on the floor with childish ill-temper.

'I only wanted to see how it might look from my point of view,' he murmured complacently.

'You did it deliberately,' she accused, 'just as you ignored me when I told you to meet me at eleven.'

'If I'd met you at eleven as you wanted, in some dark lane, and if your father had found out, what kind of construction do you think he would have put on it?' Roarke demanded. 'He would have come to the same conclusion he did this morning and hurried his plans for the wedding.'

Tisha couldn't meet the force of his gaze. There was too much truth in his statement for her to shrug it off, and he knew it.

'This way,' he went on, 'coming to the house, keeping everything open and above board, he may be persuaded to trust us.'

'What good is it going to do to have him trust us,' she

grumbled, 'if we can't get him to change his mind about this stupid marriage idea?'

'With a man like your father, you can't expect him to make an about-face overnight. You have to change his mind by degrees.'

'In other words, it will take several small miracles instead of one large one,' she murmured bitterly.

'Something like that,' Roarke agreed.

'And how do you propose to begin?' The tilt to her head challenged him to come up with an answer. 'Are you going to produce a wife out of mid-air to convince him you'd be committing bigamy if you married me now?'

'That's rather drastic,' he answered with a dry smile. 'I had thought we might convince him to extend our engagement from a few days to a few months.'

'And in those few months, he'll see how incompatible we are and agree to our breaking the engagement,' Tisha concluded for him. 'He'll never go along with it.'

'Why?'

'You don't know my father,' she grimaced. 'He's like a bulldog. Once he gets hold of an idea, he won't let go.'

'I'm sure he'll put your happiness first.'

'I'm not.' She shook her head grimly and slumped against a stool. 'He's completely discarded Kevin in favour of you. He thinks you can handle me.'

A quick glance in his direction caught the look of amusement her words aroused, a look that ignited her temper.

'This is all your fault anyway,' she declared viciously. 'If you and Dad hadn't conspired between you to make me leave this morning, we wouldn't be in this horrid predicament. Why did you let him bully you into agreeing to marry me?'

'Guilt, I suppose,' Roarke answered calmly, not the least bit upset by her sarcasm.

'Guilt?' she flared. 'There was nothing to be guilty about! Nothing happened! If you'd backed me up when I was trying to convince him of that, he might have believed us!'

'You're right. Physically nothing happened except a torrid love scene that never reached a climax.' An eyebrow quirked as his gaze roamed familiarly over her, producing again the sensation that he was touching her. 'But in my mind, let's say that it didn't end with kisses, little girl.'

His suggestive statement did not pass without a response as blood raced with disturbing swiftness to her face. At the moment his potency was too much for her to handle.

'Stop ... Stop calling me that,' she replied, fighting the breathlessness that attacked her lungs. 'I'm not a little girl.'

'No,' Roarke agreed smoothly. His hand caught a long strand of her hair. He let it spin through his fingers to fall across the agitated movement of her breasts. 'You're very much a woman, with a woman's instinctive abilities to arouse a man, as you proved last night.'

'We're ... er ... getting off the track,' Tisha stammered, turning away from him while taking a quick step to put some distance between them.

His hands settled around her waist in a provocative caress. 'I thought we were on the track.' He nuzzled her hair, following it as it flowed down her neck to her shoulders.

'Don't do that,' she protested weakly, trying to move away, only to have him hold her tighter against him.

'Why not?' he mocked. 'We're engaged. We should enjoy some of the pleasures that go along with it.'

Tisha gulped quickly for air as her resistance started to melt. She twisted in his arms, trying to use her body as a wedge to halt his searching lips.

'You forget, we're trying to find a way out of this engagement.'

'Are we?'

She saw his lazy, half-closed look dwelling on her mouth and she moistened it nervously with the tip of her tongue. An imperceptible movement of his head signalled his intention to taste the parted sweetness of her lips.

'Roarke—' she began, only to be silenced quite effectively by his kiss.

She turned the rest of the way into his arms, not sure if it was by her design or his. Her fingers were slowly inching their way towards his neck to yield completely to his embrace when there was a rap on the door followed immediately by the turning of the knob. Some sixth sense told Tisha even before she broke away from

Roarke's kiss that it would be her father in the doorway. It was his twinkling brown eyes that met the guilty darkness of her olive-green look.

'I was going to see if you two wanted some coffee,' he grinned, while Tisha attempted to struggle out of Roarke's arms without appearing to do so, but he held her easily in their circle. 'Maybe later.' And her father closed the door.

'Now you've done it!' Tisha stormed, wrenching herself free of Roarke's no longer restraining hold. 'Now we'll never be able to convince him that we don't want to get married! Why did you have to do that? I can't marry you! I just can't!'

'How was I to know your father would choose such an inopportune moment to play the host?' Roarke shrugged indifferently. 'But it's done.'

'It's done! Is that all you can say?' she raged. 'Here I am trying to figure out a way to get out of this mess while all you're doing is trying to find a way to take advantage of it! You're the most self-centred, egotistical—' She searched wildly for another deflating adjective.

'Repulsive,' he offered.

'Yes, repulsive! I couldn't stand being married to an overbearing pig like you!' she finished triumphantly.

'Do you think I want a screaming shrew of a wife hanging around my neck for the rest of my life?' he asked, studying her with a bland look. 'Although I'll admit it would be a novelty to marry someone with a split personality.'

'I don't know what you're talking about,' Tisha muttered sullenly.

'You're always so ready to hurl insults at me. Repulsive?' he mocked. 'You say you find me repulsive, yet you're always so ready to respond to my advances. Have you ever wondered why?'

'It's strictly an animal attraction.' Self-contempt lowered her chin, but it didn't take the sarcasm out of her voice. 'I'll never marry you.'

'Do you have an alternative suggestion to the one I made?'

'I'd run away before I would marry you!'

'Running never solves anything,' Roarke reminded her quietly.

'It would eliminate you as my husband,' she retorted.

'And what about your father?'

'What about him?'

'Are you prepared for the estrangement your running away would bring? The relationship between parent and child is tenuous at best. Once the bond of love and trust has been broken, it's difficult to go back. You two fight and argue now, but isn't that better than silence?'

Tisha shifted uncomfortably. She didn't need Roarke to tell her that her father was only doing what he thought was best for her. Running away would break his heart. Except for Blanche, she was the only family he had left. He loved her as much, if not more, than she loved him.

A pain-filled sigh shuddered through her. 'I don't know what to do. I love my father, but I can't marry someone just because he wants me to either.'

The hands that touched her shoulders conveyed none of the intimacy of before. Their contact was friendly and consoling as though they wanted to guide her through a dark passage into the light. She raised her eyes to his understanding smile.

'I may not have any right to ask you this, Tisha, but would you leave this to me?' Roarke asked gently. 'Would you trust me to find the solution that will make us both happy? I'm asking you to put your future in my hands.'

She searched the warm brown eyes, soft like velvet with its hidden resilience. He wanted out of this forced marriage as much as she did, she reminded herself. There was no ulterior motive to his request. What one could there be?

'Yes,' she murmured, 'I trust you.'

'Good.' He winked as if to laugh at the seriousness in her voice. 'Leave everything to me. No more arguments with your father. Say and do nothing that will make him more stubborn. The more you try to convince him that he's wrong, the more certain he'll become that he's right. Okay?'

'Okay,' she repeated, surprised that he had coaxed a smile out of her. She had thought there was nothing left to smile about. 'I bet you regret not letting me walk home last night.'

'If I'd dreamt that you had an outraged father waiting in the wings,' he chuckled, 'I would have carried you home! I might have got some sleep last night, too, instead of stiff muscles.'

'The next time something like this happens to you, you can send the girl home and sleep in your own bed,' she teased.

'There won't be any next time,' he said firmly, but with a strange enigmatic expression darkening his eyes. 'Let's take your father up on his offer of coffee before he comes back to find out what we're doing now.' His hand touched her elbow. 'And remember, leave everything to me.'

'I will, Roarke,' she promised, and wondered why she felt so secure in the hands of a man she professed not to like.

During the next few days, Tisha began to wonder if she hadn't made a mistake in trusting Roarke to find a way out of the marriage proposed by her father. Following Roarke's instructions, she had complied with all of her father's requests without a murmur of protest. Now it was Thursday and so far her father's stand hadn't taken a step in any direction except towards the marriage.

Using some influence he had, her father had rushed their blood tests through in record time. This morning their marriage licence had been obtained. Panic was beginning to set in as Tisha realized she was one step away from walking down the aisle. All her attempts to speak to Roarke alone were thwarted, mostly by her father.

Even Blanche, whom she had considered an ally, seemed to be deserting her. The rare times they had been able to talk, her aunt had plagued her with questions concerning Tisha's feelings for Roarke. Was she certain she didn't care for him? Did the physical attraction go deeper? It was obvious that Blanche considered the marriage to be inevitable.

Tisha was beginning to wonder herself. If Roarke was going to make a move, surely he would have done so by now. Her father had already made arrangements for them to be married in a local church this Saturday. Time was running out.

Slowly she trudged along the faint animal path through the forested hillside. Her father was off on some mysterious errand this afternoon and Tisha had hoped to find Roarke at home. The walk through the woods had been to confuse Blanche about her destination. The route had been longer than if she had followed the road and when she had finally reached his house, it was to find Roarke gone. Her useless hike had only succeeded in making her tired and irritable and more depressed.

Billy Goat Gruff lifted his head when she entered the clearing below her aunt's house. After a passing glance her way, he lowered his head to tear at the grass, accustomed now to her comings and goings. With a slight change of direction, Tisha headed for the kitchen door, glumly wondering how she could see Roarke tonight.

When she reached the side entrance, she glanced through the window pane of the door and saw Roarke sitting at the kitchen table with Blanche. The troubled expression on his face stopped her hand as it reached for the knob. It was eavesdropping, she knew, but she paused anyway to listen.

'Are you positive she said she was just going for a walk?' Roarke asked.

'Yes,' her aunt returned patiently, a solemn expression on her usually animated face. 'Besides, her car is still here and her clothes. I know she hasn't run away.'

Tisha wasn't certain what she thought she was going to hear, perhaps some comment that would reveal they were all conspiring to get her to marry Roarke, but they seemed to be only concerned with her whereabouts. With a resigned sigh, she opened the door and walked in.

'There you are!' Blanche rose quickly to her feet, a forced smile of brightness on her face. 'We were wondering where you'd gone.'

'First I considered throwing myself off the steepest cliff, but I couldn't find one,' said Trisha. 'Then I thought about getting lost in the woods, but I kept ending up in somebody's back yard. So here I am,' she finished bitterly.

'Don't joke about things like that,' her aunt murmured, a worried frown lining her forehead.

'I'm sorry, Blanche.' Tisha sighed wearily. 'Chalk it up to pre-wedding nerves,' darting a resentful glance at Roarke, who was watching her closely. 'And how's the prospective bridegroom?'

'Doing as well as can be expected,' he answered. His gaze followed Tisha as she walked to the counter and poured a cup of coffee. 'Grab a chair and sit down.'

'I don't feel like it!' she snapped. The combination of her own strain and his unruffled demeanour unleashed her temper.

She intercepted the look he sent Blanche, who immediately got to her feet. 'You two would probably like to be alone. I'll go and play with my paints for a while.'

As soon as she heard the studio door close behind her aunt, Tisha turned towards Roarke, her green eyes blazing with anger.

'Well? The wedding is on Saturday!'

'I know,' he answered, calmly meeting the challenge of her gaze.

'If you know, why aren't you doing something about it?' she demanded.

Very slowly, he uncoiled his long length from the chair and walked over to the counter where she stood. 'The world hasn't come to an end.' The sunlight glinted on the bronzed gold highlights in his hair.

'Not yet,' she retorted bitterly. 'I'm beginning to wonder if you have any plan at all to rescue us from this disaster.'

'I thought you were going to trust me.' The gentleness in his voice reached out to soothe her.

'I was.' Her own voice was very low, barely squeezing through the painful lump in her throat.

'That's the past tense. Does that mean you don't

trust me any more?'

Tisha looked up at him, her chin trembling as she tried to hold back the misery that was welling to the top. 'I don't know any more.'

'Hey?' His head tilted down as she lowered her chin to escape his searching eyes. Not even the teasing reassurance of his voice could raise it again. 'What happened to that little redhead who was always so positive about things? Could this be the same girl admitting that she doesn't know everything?'

'No, I don't know everything,' she admitted, breathing in deeply and rapidly to hold back the tears. In spite of all her efforts, one tear slipped from her lashes and trickled down her cheek.

'You're crying,' Roarke accused gently.

'You're darned right I'm crying!' she flared, as more tears followed the first. 'And if you were any kind of a man, you'd offer me your shoulder instead of standing there looking so righteous!'

'I didn't think you'd want my shoulder,' he mused softly, reaching out to draw her into his arms. The beat of his heart was oddly reassuring as he cradled her against his chest. His head was bowed near her forehead. 'Of course, on the other hand, I didn't realize you would give in to tears,' he murmured. 'Go ahead and cry, Tisha. It's about time you got rid of some of your independent inhibitions.'

She needed no more encouragement than that to weep freely. sparing only a fleeting thought that she was getting his shirt wet as she huddled closer to him.

When her sobs had subsided to hiccuping sounds, Roarke offered her his handkerchief, wiping the excess tears off her cheeks himself. Her head stayed nestled against his chest as she finished the rest.

'Feel better?' he asked gently.

'Yes.' Her answer was accompanied by a tiny shake of her head. 'Hold me, please,' she requested, knowing that when she left the shelter of his arms that terribly lonely feeling would descend on her.

'Gladly.' She could feel him smile against her hair while his hold tightened reassuringly around her.

'I walked up to your house to find you,' she said after a few minutes of silence.

'And I came down here to see you,' Roarke returned. One arm was removed so he could reach his hand in his pocket. 'I have something I wanted to give you.'

In the next minute, he was holding a glittering diamond solitaire ring in front of her. The size of it drew a gasp of delight from her as the sunlight was caught by its cut surface and reflected a rainbow of colours.

'Is it real?' she whispered.

'It's very real,' he mocked. 'Touch it. It won't disappear.'

Her initial elation faded. 'No,' she said firmly, moving against the back of his arm as he brought the ring closer. 'That's an engagement ring. It's beautiful, but—'

'Your father expects you to have one.'

'He expects a wedding, too,' Tisha reminded him

none too gently.

'Trust me.'

The warmth of his gaze rested on her face as she glanced warily at him. 'I'll take it,' she surrendered grudgingly. 'But I'm going to give it back to you as soon as this whole thing is over.'

Roarke slipped the ring on her finger. 'You can give it back if you want to, or keep it as a souvenir.'

'That wouldn't be right.' The ring was a perfect fit, if a little snug, and she couldn't help admiring the way it sparkled when her hand moved. 'You shouldn't have bought something so expensive. What if I lose it?'

'I had it made a little small to make it harder to get off your finger in case you threw it at me during a temper tantrum,' he mocked.

'I wouldn't do that,' she murmured, self-consciously moving out of his arms.

'Oh yes, you would,' he grinned.

'Roarke,' a worried frown swept away the glow that had been on her face, 'what are we going to do about Saturday?'

'Leave everything to me.'

'Yes, but—'

'No buts. I'll take care of everything. It will all work out for the best.'

'I wish I knew what you were going to do,' she sighed.

'Right now I'm going home – and you, stop worrying.' He touched the tip of her nose and moved towards the door. 'Tell Blanche thanks for the coffee.'

'When will I see you?'

He stopped at the door and turned around. His eyes moved over her in a touching caress that quickened her heartbeat.

'Tomorrow.'

CHAPTER NINE

By two-thirty the following afternoon, there was no sign sign of Roarke. Somehow Tisha had received the impression that when he had said he would see her tomorrow, he had meant in the afternoon. She had been clinging to the slim hope that he would arrive before her father returned from another mysterious errand, but she could hear her father greeting Blanche as he came in the door and knew that if Roarke did come now, there would be little chance to see him alone.

She wished now she had been more persistent yesterday in finding out how he intended to postpone the wedding. Twenty-four hours ago, she had trusted him. She had let his charm persuade her to leave all the details to him. Today she scolded herself for being so foolish. It was her life and she had a right to know what was going on.

The diamond on her finger sparkled brilliantly in the sunlight streaming through the skylight of the studio. A shudder quivered down her spine at the implications of marriage the ring carried. Her stomach was a mass of butterflies beating their wings against its walls. Tomorrow they were going to be married, unless he stood her up at the altar. Perhaps that was what he was planning, she thought desperately. But something like that would only enrage her father and Roarke seemed to be intent on pacifying him. If only she knew what he was planning!

'What's my little bride-to-be doing today? Working?'

At the sound of her father's voice, Tisha turned from her blank canvas. His handsome, smiling face was peering around the studio door, looking very much like a grown-up boy who had a secret he was bursting to tell. A sad smile was all she could manage to return.

'Come on in, Dad,' she invited with an absence of emotion. 'I'm not really doing anything.'

'No, you come here. I have something I want to show you,' he insisted.

Tisha wanted to refuse, but there wasn't any point in doing so. Reluctantly she followed him as he led her to her room, not really interested in whatever it was he had to show her.

'Couldn't work today, huh?' he inquired gently.

'No.'

'Don't be so dejected. It's only pre-wedding nerves,' he assured her, opening the door to her room.

'Please, Dad, I don't want to talk about it.' The tension that was pounding at the back of her head put a sharp edge to her voice.

'I bought you a present.' A gesture of his hand drew her attention to the box on the bed. 'I hope you like it.'

Tisha stared at it in a kind of frozen silence. The shape of it indicated a dress. She bit into her lower lip, knowing that if she opened it and saw a wedding dress, she would scream.

'Go on, open it,' he prodded her gently.

With trembling fingers, she slowly pulled the string off the box, trying to summon the courage to lift off the top cardboard. After an apprehensive glance at her father, she removed the top and swept aside the tissue paper. Her eyelids fluttered down in relief when she saw the tiny bouquets of blue flowers sprinkled over the white material of a dress. With a little more spirit, she unfolded it and held it up against her, the long, filmy sleeves trailing over her arm.

'It's very pretty, Daddy. Thank you,' she murmured, her lips gently touching his shaven cheek.

There was so much love shining in his eyes when he looked at her that a lump rose in her throat. He caught at her hand and looked down at it as if he too needed a moment to control his emotions. Pushing the empty box to the back of the bed, he sat down and patted the cover beside him.

'Sit down, Tish. I think it's time you and I had a little talk.'

Carefully she laid the dress over the foot of the bed and joined him near the edge. Some of her apprehension returned as she tried to anticipate what he wanted to talk about. One of his hands covered the tightly clenched fingers in her lap while the other arm moved around her shoulders to draw her against him.

He gazed tenderly into her face, a small loving smile lifting the corners of his mouth. 'I can't remember the last time that I told you how very much I love you.

Maybe it's something that parents aren't supposed to tell their children. It's taken for granted, I suppose. But I wanted to say it out loud. I wanted you to know how very much you mean to me.'

Tears sprang to her eyes. 'Oh, Daddy, I love you, too,' Tisha whispered as his arm tightened in an affectionate hug.

'After you were born and your mother and I found out she couldn't have any more children, she felt that she'd let me down by not giving me a son. I don't believe I ever convinced her that I was satisfied with the beautiful child of our love. Oh, I did want a son — every man does. But you were never second best, honey,' her father assured her, his hand stroking the head that rested against his shoulder. 'If I could have traded you in for a boy the minute you were born, I wouldn't have done it. Do you believe me?'

'Yes.' The simple answer erased the little frown that had gathered on his forehead.

'I want you to be happy, but sometimes I know I've gone about it in all the wrong ways. There were many times when I should have been more understanding, but I'd never been a parent before.'

'I wouldn't have traded you for anyone.' Tisha hadn't felt so close to her father in years. She couldn't even bring herself to be angry over his high-handed treatment that was forcing her into marriage with Roarke.

'These last few days,' he went on, 'I've had several opportunities to talk to Roarke. He's very concerned that I'm rushing you into something you aren't prepared for.'

Unconsciously Tisha held her breath. Was this the moment? Was this when her father would agree to the long engagement that Roarke wanted?

'Last Sunday, my temper ruled my judgment,' he went on. 'Your welfare was all that concerned me. When my anger cooled, I had second doubts that I hadn't done the wise thing, that I'd acted too hastily. But after talking to him and realizing how much he wants your happiness to be placed first, I know he'll be a better husband for you than I had a right to expect.'

Her heart plunged to the pit of her stomach. It hadn't worked! The wedding was not going to be postponed. A thousand cries of protest rose in her throat, but none escaped her tightly drawn lips. Tisha had only one thought – to tell Roarke his plan had failed. They had only a few short hours to come up with another one.

'Are you very angry with me for making all the arrangements for the wedding without consulting you?' her father asked gently.

'No,' she answered truthfully. What did she care about a ceremony that was never going to take place, even if she had to run away to prevent it?

'When your mother and I were married, we had an enormous wedding,' he told her. 'She was an only child, too, but her parents insisted on making a production of it, every great-aunt and uncle and fourth cousin was invited. The celebration lasted all day and probably all night, but we slipped away before it was over.'

He paused, his eyes taking on a faraway look as if he were reliving the precious memory of that day.

Some seconds later, he continued, his voice low and unbelievably tender, 'When we'd driven some distance, I remember Lenore said she wished the ceremony had never happened. I was stunned at first because I thought she was regretting marrying me. Then she explained that she felt our love was a precious blessing from God, a private, beautiful emotion that wasn't meant to be flaunted. There were tears in her eyes when she told me that she wished it could have only been the two of us standing in front of the altar without all the bridesmaids and groomsmen around, only the two of us exchanging our holy vows in God's house. We happened to be driving through a small town when she told me this. I saw a church with the lights on and we stopped. We made our vows a second time in front of a simple altar with rows of empty pews behind us. We loved each other, Tisha, more than words can ever say.'

His voice cracked as he took her face in his hands and stared into it, a poignant sadness in his eyes.

'And that is why, my darling, darling daughter,' he murmured tightly, 'your wedding to Roarke is going to be so simple. Not because I want to hide anything or make it a hurry-up affair. It was the second time that we pledged our love that your mother and I treasured. For you I want it to be the first, with no other memory to detract from it.'

She turned her face in his hands, pressing a kiss against his palm, a conflicting tide of emotions swamping her. How could she tell him that she couldn't go through with the ceremony he planned?

'I never realized completely how much you loved my mother,' her voice still smothered in his hand.

'She loved me, too,' he whispered, gathering her against his chest. 'Seeing you with Roarke this last week has reminded me of it so vividly. Whenever he's around you hardly take your eyes off of him. You're constantly sending little messages to him the way Lenore used to do with me. I bet you didn't think your old dad noticed things like that, did you?' She could feel him smile against her forehead and frowned. 'I realized last night that the biggest reason you don't want to marry him, or say you don't want to marry him, is because of the speed at which it's all happening, as if the two of you had done something to be ashamed of last week-end. I know you didn't.'

'What?' Tisha breathed.

'You've never lied to me, honey, and you didn't when you told me nothing had happened. I've already seen for myself that Roarke respects you too much to have taken advantage of the situation. I know it's terribly old-fashioned to say that I'm glad you waited, but I am. Do you remember a couple of weeks ago?' he chuckled, and gently held her away from him. 'It seems longer than that. But you told me that I would never approve of the man you married, that I would find something wrong with him. You were wrong. Roarke might even be too good for you, but I doubt it. You couldn't have made a better choice if you'd searched the whole world. I'm not only going to have a daughter I adore, but a son-in-law, too. A father couldn't be any luckier than that.'

Tisha could only stare at him in dumb amazement. None of this was happening to her. She was overwhelmed. There seemed to be no arguments left. Her mind refused to think.

Her father glanced down at his watch and shook his head wryly. 'Here I've been rambling on and paying no attention to the time. We have to be at the church in forty-five minutes, and you haven't had a chance to try the dress on to see if it fits.'

The rehearsal, she thought dejectedly as she got to her feet. At least Roarke would be there. She would have her chance to see him and reveal her father's new stand. She picked up the dress and fingered the material of the flared skirt.

'Did . . . did you want me to wear this?' she asked hesitantly.

'Slacks would hardly be appropriate,' he smiled. 'Can you be ready in fifteen minutes?'

'Yes,' Tisha nodded.

As she absently changed into the dress, her mind kept flitting back over her father's words. His expression of love for her moved her even as it seemed to trap her. The alternatives had been narrowed down to one – flight. The tragedy was that her father was convinced she loved Roarke.

It was true that she looked at him a lot. His presence had a way of dominating a room. But she told herself that she looked at him because he promised a way out. He, too, was trapped into marrying her. That was the bond that held them, not the love that her father saw.

Adding a touch of light blue shadow to intensify the green of her eyes, Tisha stepped back from the mirror to stare at her reflection. Tension had produced a starry, ethereal quality in her face. Nerves had knotted her stomach until she wanted to press her hands against it to relieve the pain. Subconsciously she knew the dress was particularly flattering to her while the rest of her thoughts kept praying that Roarke could come up with a solution for their latest crisis.

When she walked into the living-room, she only half noticed her father had changed out of his sports clothes into a suit and that Blanche was there looking very chic in a red suit. An absent smile curved her mouth when her father took her hand and carried it to his lips.

'You look beautiful, Patricia,' he said with intense sincerity.

She nodded at his compliment and replied with the thought that was uppermost in her mind, 'We'd better hurry or we'll be late.' She was driven by the compulsion to see Roarke as quickly as possible.

Yet the short journey into Hot Springs seemed to take forever. Small talk would have made it impossible, but luckily neither her father nor Blanche commented on her silence.

Her legs threatened not to support as she walked

beside her father into the empty vestibule of the church. She glanced anxiously around for Roarke, knowing he was here somewhere because she had seen his car outside. Tisha didn't notice her father turn to Blanche and take something from her. When he walked over to her and gently draped a lace scarf over her hair, she looked at him impatiently.

'I don't need to wear anything over my head, do I?' she protested.

'You should have something,' he insisted quietly, wrapping the long tails around her neck and over her shoulder.

He took her hand and tucked it under his arm, winking at her in reassurance. The doors to the interior of the church were opened and she willingly fell in step with him as he walked towards it. She would rather have seen Roarke before the rehearsal, she thought nervously. They had only taken two short steps into the aisle itself when she saw Roarke standing at the altar waiting with the minister. The look in his eyes nearly buckled her knees. Her fingers curled into her father's arm as she stared at his solemn expression.

'This . . .' Panic nearly robbed her of her voice. 'This isn't a rehearsal, is it?' she whispered, making it more of a statement than a question.

He shifted his arm so that it was supporting her waist as he kept her moving down the aisle closer to Roarke.

'Of course not,' he replied, as if she should have known it all along.

Her wide, frightened gaze was captured by the tenderly serious light of Roarke's. There was a hint of apology in their dark depths as he accepted her trembling hand from her father. Roarke, too, encircled her waist with his arm, holding her upright when her quivering legs threatened to collapse. Her lips parted, wanting to speak, to halt the ceremony in some way, but the minister had already begun his intonation.

'Dearly beloved, we—'

It was too late. Tisha knew it in her heart as she listened to the words that joined her in marriage to the man beside her. With a bowed head, she repeated her vows in a barely audible voice. Only when she had uttered the last words did she look into his face. Stained glass windows intensified the gold highlights in his hair while his eyes watched the movement of her mouth as she pledged herself to him.

The clear, resonant sound of his voice vibrated through her, removing the blindfold she had been wearing and allowing her to see the sunburst that radiated from her heart. With almost terrifying certainty, Tisha knew she was in love with Roarke. Every clamouring beat of her heart was for him.

She not only physically belonged to him, but mentally as well. Not by any legal act, but because she wanted to be. She wanted to share his life, have his children, grow old in his arms.

For a moment Tisha almost believed that he wanted it too, until she remembered the unwillingness he had voiced to marry her. Her father had manoeuvred them into this ceremony. Roarke didn't want to marry her.

He had been forced to do so to prevent a scandal. How could any marriage survive in those circumstances? It couldn't, answering the question herself. Legally they were going to be man and wife, but it was a situation he would change at the earliest possible moment.

If Roarke should ever guess she was in love with him? The thought struck a cold chill in her heart. He would certainly believe that she had been a part of the conspiracy to marry him. How he would hate her for that!

She stared at the gold band he had placed on her finger. The diamond in her engagement ring sparkled with multi-coloured light beside the plain gold of her wedding ring. That was what she wanted – the rainbow and the moon – and both were equally out of reach without Roarke's love.

'By the authority vested in me, I now pronounce you man and wife. You may kiss the bride,' the minister prompted.

Her lashes fluttered down to close her eyes. The pain inside was much too intense to be able to withstand the resignation that must be in Roarke's face as he gently turned her to face him. There was no ardour in his kiss, none of the warmth that she usually felt. His touch was cool and controlled as though he was obliged to carry out the minister's instructions.

Numbly she heard the words of congratulations extended to Roarke and thought of the bitterness he must feel accepting them as he had accepted her, a wife he didn't want. The embrace of her father and his obvious happiness couldn't reach her soul, which seemed to have died, nor the whispered wish of her aunt that she and Roarke would be happy.

Her hand touched the dark sleeve of his suit. She hadn't looked at him since she had realized she was in love with him, but she did so now. The face he turned towards her was serious and a little guarded.

'Please,' Tisha said hoarsely in a voice so low he had to bend down to hear her, 'let's get out of here.'

'Of course,' came his clipped reply.

In seconds he had bustled her away from her father and Blanche and was escorting her down the church steps to his car. She desperately wanted to flee in the opposite direction, but she had to face him some time. Above all, she had to convince him that she didn't want to be married to him any more than he wanted to be married to her. Pride would not let her use the legal bonds of matrimony to hold him.

'You didn't know your father had changed the wedding from tomorrow to today, did you?' Roarke said as he slid behind the wheel of the car.

'No.' she answered shortly, her voice raw with pain. 'I didn't know any more than you did.'

He shot her an inquiring look before switching on the motor. 'We're married now.'

'It's a mockery and you know it!' she declared bitterly.

'What do you suggest? An early annulment?' he asked. centring his gaze on the traffic around them.

'Surely it's the obvious solution.'

'Is it?' he returned cryptically.

'I should never have believed you,' she murmured angrily, tearing the lace scarf from her head. 'If I hadn't listened to you, we wouldn't be in this mess,' adding to herself that she might not have discovered that she loved him and avoided this heartbreak.

'Do you make a habit out of crying over spilt milk?' he asked.

'I'm not so foolish as to believe that things always turn out for the best,' Tisha shot back.

'It turns out for the best if you make it,' Roarke answered calmly. 'It's a case of turning disadvantage into advantage.'

'That may be true in business, but how do you turn an unwanted marriage into a wanted marriage?' she demanded.

'That sounds like a pretty impossible task,' he agreed, turning the car into the car-park of a hotel.

'What are we doing here?' she demanded.

His glance mocked the apprehension in her voice. 'I didn't want to test your cooking. The mood you're in you would probably try to poison me. And things always look better on a full stomach.'

'I'm not hungry,' she avowed, not finding any humour in his statement.

'We'll have a drink first. Maybe some of the shock of becoming Mrs. Madison will wear off and your appetite will return.'

'You don't mean shock, you mean horror,' Tisha snapped.

'You see,' Roarke grinned with a lifted brow, 'it's

169

already beginning. Whenever you start insulting me, I know things are back to normal.'

There wasn't any 'normal' any more, Tisha thought as she watched Roarke get out of the car and walk around to open her door. There was heaven and hell with nothing in between except misery. But she could hide her love for him behind the sting of her tongue. It was the only defence she had left to keep from throwing herself at his feet and begging him to let her stay at his side for ever.

'Did Father plan our honeymoon, too?' she jeered, stepping quickly away from the hand that reached to guide her.

'He left it up to us. I had the impression that he didn't think we would care where we were.'

A bitter laugh came shrilly from her throat. 'We wouldn't – as long as we weren't together.'

'It would be a little difficult in the circumstances, don't you think?' His voice was suddenly grim as his fingers dug into her arms.

'Why?' She paid no heed to the warning in his gaze. 'We could have a modern honeymoon. You go your way and I'll go mine.'

A mask slipped over his face. 'And let your husband sleep alone on his wedding night?' he clicked his tongue in mockery. 'Shame on you, Red!'

A terrifying numbness paralysed her. 'Is that how you plan to take advantage of the disadvantage of our marriage? Do you intend to claim your rights?'

'The thought occurred to me,' he answered

smoothly, his eyes moving possessively over her.

'Well, you can forget it!' she declared with a rush, her whole body pulsating with a wild heat at the thought of his lovemaking.

'You appeared to be willing last week,' he reminded her. 'Why this sudden attack of conscience when it would be morally permitted?'

A crimson glow stained her face. 'For as long as this marriage lasts, it will be in name only.' Her voice trembled with determination.

'Now that we're married you no longer find me attractive, is that right?'

'No.' The denial was out before she could stop it.

'That means I still disturb you physically, then.'

'Yes ... I mean no!'

'What do you mean?' A glint of arrogant humour was in his gaze.

'I ... I mean,' Tisha fought for the breath that was being denied her, 'that this farcical marriage is going no farther. It's ... it's a total sham!'

'That means you don't want any Bermudan honeymoon, then.'

'No, I don't.' Tisha shook her head firmly.

'I suppose the most logical thing to do is to return to my home when we've eaten. Do you agree?' He seemed suddenly disinclined to argue with her and Tisha was glad. His sly questions were beginning to destroy her resolve not to make a further mockery of their marriage.

'That's fine,' she nodded.

CHAPTER TEN

TISHA didn't know if her appetite had really returned or whether she took such a long time over each course to prolong the inevitable moment when they would be alone. The silence between them was neither comfortable nor uneasy, broken occasionally by idle comments to avoid any building tension. After a second cup of coffee following dessert, Tisha knew she had lingered as long as possible.

Roarke did, too. He motioned for the waitress to bring their bill. 'Are you ready?' It was a polite question, since he knew the answer.

The intimate darkness of night had descended outside with only a few stars shimmering in the distance. The moon was new, a pale sickle against a black background. And Tisha was more conscious than ever of the close confines of the sports car. Yet Roarke seemed to pay no attention to her as he silently drove through the empty country roads.

The nervous tension that had been absent during the meal came with shaking swiftness to take hold of her as they neared his house. The lights of her aunt's house winked at her through the pines, then they were turning down the lane to Roarke's house.

She stood nervously beside him as he unlocked the front door, catching the mocking glance he tossed at her when he opened the door and waited for her to precede him.

'I don't want to make it a further mockery by carrying you over the threshold,' he murmured.

'Of course,' she agreed tightly, stepping quickly by him into the foyer. Her memories of her last visit were all too vivid. When Roarke flicked the light on, she saw the suitcases sitting by the door and recognized them as her own. 'What are these doing here?'

'Blanche must have brought a few of your clothes up for you,' he replied, without any show of surprise. 'She probably thought you would want to wear something other than your wedding dress in the next couple of days.' He reached down and picked up her cases. 'I'll take them into the bedroom for you.'

There seemed to be nothing else to do except follow him as he entered the living-room, his supple stride carrying him unhurriedly ahead of her. A fire was blazing in the fireplace and the lights were turned down low. Tisha stopped at the bottom of the steps, her green eyes spying the magnum of champagne on ice and the two stemmed glasses on the tray beside it.

'How did that get here?' she demanded icily. He glanced over his shoulder, his gaze following her pointing finger to the champagne. Amusement curled the corners of his mouth.

'It looks like a gift from your father to celebrate our wedding night. There's no sense in letting it go to waste. Why don't you open it up while I put your things in the other room?'

He didn't wait for a reply to his suggestion and resumed his course to the bedroom, the suitcases under his arm. Tisha walked stiffly to the couch, staring angrily at the wine bottle and the pair of glasses. Her imagination filled in the scene that was supposed to transpire as she and Roarke sat in front of the cosy fire, sipping champagne. She was still staring at the bottle when he walked back into the room.

'Haven't you opened it?' he asked unnecessarily.

'I don't know how,' she swallowed nervously, avoiding the couch in favour of a chair.

Covertly she watched as he expertly uncorked the bottle and allowed no bubbling foam to escape. He turned the glasses over and let his eyes ask the question of her.

'I don't want any,' she answered shortly.

'Suit yourself,' he shrugged, pouring a glass for himself.

With a casualness Tisha wished she had, he removed his suit jacket and loosened his tie before settling down on the couch. When he picked up a newspaper and began leafing through it, she couldn't make up her mind if he was ignoring her deliberately or whether her presence didn't bother him at all. The last was a sharp jolt to her ego since she found him uncomfortably disturbing.

'How can you sit there and read?' Tisha exclaimed in exasperation. 'Isn't there something you can do?'

'Like what?' He folded one side of the paper back so he could look at her.

'Like figuring a way to end this absurd marriage!'

'It's a bit premature for that.' The newspaper was raised to block out his face.

'Why?' she persisted.

'We both know your father would never accept it as final if we attempted to separate tomorrow morning.'

'How long will we have to wait?' There was hardly any colour in her face as she waited for his answer.

'A few months.'

'What happens in the meantime?' she swallowed.

The newspaper was folded and laid on the couch beside him while he cocked his head and looked at her curiously. 'I'm not sure I know what you mean.'

'I mean where will you and I be during these few months?' Her fingers were nervously twisting themselves in knots in her lap.

'We'll be right here.' An amused frown mocked her for not seeing the obvious.

'In this house?' Despair brought her to her feet. 'That's impossible!'

'Why?'

Her hands swept around her in a hopeless gesture. 'It's so small. We'd be constantly tripping over each other.'

'I don't understand the relevance of that statement,' Roarke murmured, leaning against the back of the couch and folding his arms complacently in front of him.

'You know very well what I'm talking about,' she accused angrily.

'Are you concerned that constant contact would weaken your resolve to keep this marriage – what was that quaint phrase you used? Oh, yes, in name only?' The lines around his mouth deepened.

'Considering the mess we're in, it's the only logical way. There would be undisputable grounds for divorce. We agreed to that!' Tisha announced in a desperate voice.

'I know you said that's the way it was going to be, but I don't recall agreeing to it.'

His answer froze her. He was teasing her, that was all, she told herself as she searched his face to be sure she was right.

'Will you stop making fun of me?' she muttered, biting her lip as she turned towards the fire.

'You're too nervous,' he declared. 'Why don't you reconsider and have a glass of champagne?'

The grate of ice against the bottle was followed by the sound of liquid being poured into a glass. Then Roarke was beside her holding out the partially filled glass.

'Shall we drink a toast to the happy bride and groom?' he suggested mockingly.

Her eyes glittered angrily as she watched him sip his own drink. His amusement at the whole situation irritated her more than his indifference.

'I would rather drink to our imminent separation,' she vowed in a low, trembling voice.

To enforce her statement, she swallowed almost the entire contents of the glass, her fingers gripping the stem so tightly that with the slightest addition of pressure it would have snapped.

'This is good wine. It's meant to be sipped, not gulped,' he chided. Rebelliously Tisha swallowed the rest and glared at him, longing to throw the empty glass into the fireplace as a final show of determination. 'Whatever you do,' he murmured, correctly interpreting the gleam in her eyes, 'please don't throw that glass at the fireplace. It would take you for ever to get all the splintered particles out of the carpet.'

'What makes you think I would try?' she demanded, tossing her head back.

'You're the woman of the house now. Keeping it clean is usually the wife's chore,' Roarke shrugged, leisurely moving away from her.

'You'd like that, wouldn't you?' she spat. 'That's why you're looking forward to keeping me around for a few months, so you can have free maid service, and a cook, and all those other things.'

'I doubt that it will be free. You'll probably demand an enormous allowance,' he murmured.

'I want nothing from you!' Tisha stormed. 'Not your name or your money!'

'What do you want?' he asked quietly, his eyes narrowing ever so slightly as he looked at her.

Her throat constricted with pain. She wanted his love, but she could never tell him that. Instead she drew herself up proudly.

'To be left alone.' With an imperious turn, she started for the hallway, finding it impossible to continue fielding his comments.

'Where are you going?' Roarke asked with a bland show of interest.

'To bed,' she tossed over her shoulder.

'It's a little early, isn't it?'

'It's only nine o'clock,' she agreed, 'but I have to unpack and shower yet.

'It has been a rather hectic, nerve-racking day,' he admitted. 'It probably wouldn't hurt to turn in early.'

'For once we agree,' she murmured sarcastically, and hurried down the hall before he could reply in kind.

Her suitcases were sitting on the floor at the foot of the bed. She had no intention of unpacking them since she was determined not to remain very long in the house, certainly not the few months that Roarke had mentioned. The line of her mouth tightened grimly as she searched through the cases for her pyjamas. But Blanche had only packed a slinky silk nightgown that clung suggestively to her curves.

Taking it, a blue robe and the nightcase with her cosmetics, Tisha scurried into the bathroom adjoining the master bedroom, trying very hard not to recall the last time she had been in there. At least she wouldn't have to wear Roarke's pyjamas this time, she thought wryly as she stepped into the shower stall to adjust the water temperature.

A quarter of an hour later, she was dressed in her nightgown and had slipped on the covering robe before opening the door into the bedroom. As she stepped into the room, she saw Roarke standing on the other side of the bed, unbuttoning his shirt.

'What are you doing here?' Tisha breathed, her eyes widening as he removed his shirt.

'I decided you had the right idea about making it an early night,' he returned smoothly.

'You're not sleeping in here?' It was meant to be a statement, but the uncertainty in her voice made it a question.

One brow was raised in mockery before he turned to sit on the bed, his back to her. 'I'm not about to spend another night trying to sleep on the couch.'

'Well, I will, then, because I am not going to share a bed with you!' Tisha declared, moving hurriedly towards the door, afraid at any moment to feel Roarke's hand on her arm.

A glance over her shoulder as she opened the door into the hall revealed that he was still sitting on the bed, now removing his shoes. Worst of all, she felt disappointed that he hadn't tried to make her stay. Some weak part of her wanted her objections to be swept aside.

Inside the study, Tisha stared at the couch, realizing she had forgotten to get any pillows or blankets, but reluctant to return to the room where Roarke was in case she gave in to any last-minute persuasions. Sleep was impossible anyway, she decided, walking aimlessly about the room.

A stereo record player was enclosed in a cabinet on the far side of the room. Leafing through the phonograph albums stacked next to it, she chose one and put it on the turntable. She returned to curl on to the couch as violins cried a melancholy tune. Drawing her knees up to her chest, she cradled her chin on them and listened to the sad melodies that matched the sorrow in her heart.

A shadow fell across the steps. Her muscles stiffened as she raised her head to stare at Roarke. Her pulse was beating a wild tattoo in her throat at the implacably calm expression in his face.

'What are you doing here?' she demanded in a wary tone.

The dark eyes swept over her before he mounted the steps and walked towards the stereo wailing in the corner.

'I'm not going to stay awake tonight listening to lonely violins,' he answered, flicking off the switch.

She was sure that he could hear the pounding of her heart in the ensuing silence. She tried to appear as calm and in control as Roarke did.

'Would you bring me a pillow and some blankets?' she requested icily.

'No.'

His reply was spoken so quietly that at first Tisha didn't realize what he had said. When it did sink in, she unconsciously tilted her chin at a defiant angle.

'What do you mean?'

'I mean that you won't need them,' Roarke answered, still standing in the shadowy corner near the record player where it was difficult to see his face.

'Why? Have you decided to sleep here instead?' she asked, maintaining a hostile façade with a concerted effort.

Slowly his footsteps eliminated the distance between them until he was standing in front of her, his unrelenting eyes holding hers captive.

'No. And neither are you.'

There was an agitated shake of her head. 'I'm not spending the night with you.' Her voice trembled, making her words uncertain.

'Yes, you are,' Roarke answered smoothly, reaching down to draw her to her feet. 'So stop arguing.'

Tisha tried to pull away from his grip. 'No, I'm not! I don't want to!' There was panic in her voice.

'And stop lying.' One corner of his mouth quirked in a humourless smile. 'Don't try to pretend that you don't want me as I want you.'

'No! No! Please . . .' As she increased her struggle to free herself, he smoothly picked her up and carried her in his arms down the steps, through the door into the hall. 'Put me down!' she gasped, uselessly kicking her feet in the air while one arm was pinned by her own body against his chest and the other was restrained by Roarke. 'I don't want to go to bed with you! I don't want you to touch me! This isn't part of our agreement!'

'There was no agreement,' he informed her. 'You were the only one who assumed there was.'

The bedroom door was open and Roarke carried her in, closing it with his foot. Out of the corner of her eye,

Tisha saw the bed, its covers turned down, and she wiggled against the firmness of his hold.

'Stop it! Put me down!' Her cry was only a forlorn hope now as he carried her down the steps. 'You're a hateful, unprincipled beast!' she accused uselessly. 'I'm not some Sabine woman to be dragged into your bedroom to satisfy your animal desires!'

With an amused sigh, he set her on her feet, his hands still holding her arms at her side, while his eyes mocked her little attempts to twist free.

'There's only one way to silence you, isn't there?' he smiled.

And he pulled her hard against his chest, halting the vitriolic flow of insults with a conquering kiss. For a moment, Tisha was able to resist the assault on her senses, but his ardour was much too determined and persuasive and she could no longer keep her love bottled up.

With a surrendering sigh, she slipped her arms around his neck, no longer fighting his attempts to mould her closer as she gave herself up to the rapture and fire of his touch. While his mouth sensually explored her neck and the hollow of her throat, she yielded gladly when his hands slipped the robe from her shoulders.

As his fingers touched the shoulder strap of her nightgown, Tisha knew there was no turning back. And there was exultant gladness in knowing she didn't want to either.

'Roarke,' she whispered. The ache for him was in

her voice. 'I want you to know I love you.'

'I guessed that all along,' he murmured against her mouth.

'Roarke—'

'You talk too much,' he declared, lifting her again into his arms and carrying her to the bed, his mouth effectively shutting off any more attempts at conversation.

Later in the night he turned to her again, and this time Tisha offered no token resistance to his desire. There was none of the pain of before as he aroused her to the fullest delights of womanhood.

When the morning sunlight awakened her, she slipped quietly from the bed, glancing briefly at Roarke's slumbering form as she picked up the robe from the floor to hide her nakedness. The bliss that had so tenderly enveloped her last night was gone, replaced by the sobering memory that Roarke had not wanted to marry her.

Staring out the window, Tisha tried to hate him for taking advantage of the situation, for making her his wife in deed as well as in word. He had admitted that he had guessed that she loved him and had used the power this gave him to satisfy his own needs. Yet the light of day didn't lessen her desire to spend the rest of her life with him. And Roarke was planning to file for a divorce in a few months. Tisha never realized how humiliating it was to want someone who didn't want you.

Never would she beg to stay! Last night she had been weak. Today she had to be strong and all the days that followed this one. Her pride would have to conceal the depth of her love because she could never tolerate his pity.

She turned from the window, her gaze hungrily seeking the masculine figure in the bed. He was awake, lazily watching her with a dark light in his eyes that immediately sent an answering rush of fire through her blood. But Tisha determinedly tilted her chin.

'Good morning,' she greeted him coolly.

Roarke propped himself upright on one elbow, arching a brow as he searched her face. 'Good morning,' he returned, his eyes narrowing slightly. 'We must have had a cold front move in during the night.'

She ignored his innuendo at her frigid greeting. 'I'm going to make some coffee. If you want any, you can come out to the kitchen and get it.'

To get from the window to the steps leading to the door, Tisha had to go by the bed. Even though she was prepared for some movement from him to prevent her, she still wasn't able to elude the hand that closed over her wrist.

'What's the matter with you?' he demanded. The covers fell back, revealing the bareness of his muscular, tanned chest while she fought the intoxication of his touch.

'I don't want any morning romp in the bed, so let go of my arm,' she answered sarcastically.

There was a disbelieving frown beneath the tousled light brown hair on his forehead. 'What happened to the loving woman I held in my arms last night?'

'Last night was a mistake!' There was an angry tremor in her voice. 'And it's a mistake that won't be repeated!'

With a vicious yank, he pulled her on to the bed beside him, his eyes narrowing dangerously as he searched her rebellious face. Tisha lay rigidly beside him, not fighting nor attempting to escape.

'What is it? Are you ashamed of what happened between us last night?' Roarke muttered.

'Yes!' the clipped affirmative striking out at him more effectively than her hands.

'For God's sake, why? We're married.'

'Let's not go into the legality of what happened,' she replied swiftly and with freezing derision.

'You can't forget it either,' he reminded her.

'Nor can I forget that you were forced to marry me with Father figuratively standing behind you with a shotgun!' Tisha retorted.

She saw the savage light go out of Roarke's eyes as he threw back his head and laughed. Her breath was caught by the engaging smile on his face when he brought a tender gaze back to her face.

'That's what's bothering you, isn't it?' he murmured, the smouldering fires in his eyes making her heart race.

'It was a low, contemptible thing you did last night, taking advantage of the situation and me,' she snapped, swallowing back the longing that rose in her throat.

'Why is it contemptible to make love to my wife —

who enjoyed it very much? Didn't she?' His lips followed her jaw-line in a feathery caress.

'Don't change the subject!' She forced herself to remain immobile even as he found the pulsing cord in her neck. My father forced you to marry me!'

'No one – with the possible exception of you – has ever forced me to do anything, Patricia Caldwell Madison,' Roarke said firmly, abandoning his exploration to gaze into her glittering eyes.

'Do you deny that you were an unwilling party to our marriage?' she demanded angrily.

'I deny it most emphatically,' he answered. Tisha stared at him in open-mouthed surprise. 'Has the cat finally got your tongue?' he teased with an impish grin.

'Are you saying ... Do you mean ...' She was terrified to put the question into words for fear she was misunderstanding him.

'I am saying and I meant that I love you, that I wanted to marry you, that I wanted some day to feel our children growing inside you, and that it's you I want to see in the rocking chair beside me when we've both grown old together.'

There was an exquisite sob of pleasure at his tender and unmistakable declaration of love.

'Then why ... Daddy ...' Her thoughts were going in so many directions that she couldn't get the questions out. 'You were going to postpone the marriage.'

'Only because I wanted you to be sure you loved me.' His fingers traced the outline of her mouth. 'All of this would have been much less complicated if your father hadn't shown up last week. It put you on the defensive. I thought a long engagement would give you time to admit that you loved me, but your father didn't see the need. And the day I gave you the ring, I was certain beyond any doubt that you loved me. You aren't the type to put your happiness in another person's hands unless you love them.'

'I do love you, Roarke. I finally admitted it to myself at the church when we took our vows,' she murmured, not even aware that her hands were creeping around his neck. 'I just couldn't believe that you loved me.'

'Well, you can stop doubting it,' he ordered.

'I think,' she whispered, brushing her lips teasingly against his while a mischievous light of happiness sparkled in her eyes, 'that you may have to spend the rest of your life proving it to me.'

'It will be my pleasure,' Roarke answered. His arms brought her closer in his embrace. 'I hope you're not determined to make that coffee now.'

'What coffee?' Tisha smiled, meeting his lips eagerly as his head moved down to hers.

Harlequin Romance

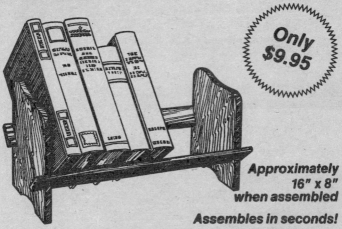